Tod slipped his arm around her

"I've much to tell you, Christabel, some of it not good. But don't let it rob us of the sweetness of this moment." He kissed her lingeringly, then spoke urgently. "You like me a little, Christabel, don't you? Enough to bear with me when I tell you some things you won't like? And forgive me?"

Christabel pushed him away, her eyes searching. "What can you mean? It's late, you said you'd rather tell me when we get back to London. I've had doubts about your life in New Zealand, but I'm inclined to trust you."

She was caught against him, kissed passionately. Then finally Tod spoke. "It's time we got back. After all, we've plenty of time ahead of us."

But Tod was quite, quite wrong.

ESSIE SUMMERS
is also the author of these
Harlequin Romances

Many of these books are available at your local bookseller.

For a free catalog listing all titles currently available,
send your name and address to:

HARLEQUIN READER SERVICE
1440 South Priest Drive, Tempe, AZ 85281
Canadian address: Stratford, Ontario N5A 6W2

Daughter of the Misty Gorges

by

ESSIE SUMMERS

Harlequin Books

TORONTO • NEW YORK • LOS ANGELES • LONDON
AMSTERDAM • PARIS • SYDNEY • HAMBURG
STOCKHOLM • ATHENS • TOKYO • MILAN

Original hardcover edition published in 1981
by Mills & Boon Limited

ISBN 0-373-02525-4

Harlequin Romance first edition January 1983

CHAPTER ONE

Now was the time, Christabel knew, when she must create a new life for herself, to stop looking back with wistfulness to the days of their family life and to put zest into her future. She had always known, as she had been born late in life to her parents, that she could be on her own early enough.

She had already conquered that feeling of utter desolation that had possessed her at first . . . now she could turn the key in her flat door and enter without a fierce longing to hear her mother's voice or her father's. They had wanted it that way, that she shouldn't grieve too long.

'Life is for getting on with,' her father had said, 'and you've got what it takes, Christabel, and, just as I did, you'll find great compensation in your writing. Then, in good time, I hope you'll find in marriage what your mother and I found. I'd like to have known the man of your choice, oh, how I would, but I'll rely on you to be discriminating. Above all, don't resent this—that I should follow your mother so soon. Don't resent any experience life brings, just use it. Don't let anything cramp your talent, love. I did, long ago, when my first wife died. It was wrong to tell myself I *couldn't* write. I think if I'd overcome it sooner, I might have had more to leave you now, but there'll be enough for you to perhaps work just part-time and to put the rest into your writing. I'm egotistical enough to want to be missed a little, *at first*. But then get on with life, girl.'

So she had got on with it, and a heady sense of achievement was hers. Recently her first book had been accepted. A pang tore through her at the thought that there was no one of her very own to share with her that moment of supreme triumph. As second-best she had written off the glorious news to her half-sister Lisa, now living in New Zealand. She had thought Lisa would cable her congratulations, might even telephone her across those thirteen thousand miles, because Lisa's husband didn't exactly have to count the bawbees, but she had not even written back very promptly. She had waited three weeks before sending that airmail letter. Oh well, that was Lisa. Yet it took only five or six days from London to reach that lonely sheep station tucked in among the highest mountains of that country of many soaring heights.

Since then, weeks and weeks ago, she had not heard another word. Perhaps Lisa was sulking because Christabel hadn't gone out, as she had suggested, to be with her. Christabel hadn't thought it wise. It wouldn't have been easy for Lisa's Rogan to become husband to Lisa and stepfather to Davina and Hughie, and would have been harder still had she introduced a half-sister into the household. It just didn't work, that sort of thing; it never had, from time immemorial. Lisa would accept in time that her young sister was carving out a career for herself, and that that career lay in London, not a country at the bottom of the world. And Dad had set his face against it. He had said that this time Lisa must learn to stand on her own feet, take full responsibility for her children, not lean on Christie. 'She'll be far happier that way, and so will Rogan. He won't spoil her as poor Jamie did. He'll expect a wife who'll pull her weight.'

Anyway, that was all in the past now ... her foot was on the first rung. With her father's legacy, plus what she had saved at her secretarial post, and doing her own writing only at nights and weekends, she had been able to resign from her position, and after this coach tour of the south-west counties and Wales, she would be writing full-time, knowing the joy of the dew-fresh inspiring hours of the morning were hers in which to create her stories. When she had completed her second novel, she was going to buy a small car and tour round at her own whim, seeking out settings for future books. This touring, with a bunch of people, was only a second-best.

Janice, her closest friend, had approved. 'It's better,

anyway, if you must retire from the hub of things, to be with people on your travels. You could easily become a hermit, a loner, get obsessed with this mode of life.'

Christabel had chuckled, 'What you mean is that you're afraid I won't meet any men! How transparent you are, pet. It comes from being so happily married yourself . . . you can't imagine any other existence. But time to myself, with no one to worry about, is going to satisfy me for ages.'

'Oh, I wouldn't want Lisa still hung round your neck like an Old Man of the Sea, I'd rather loneliness any time than that, for you. Best thing she ever did was to marry someone at the other side of the world . . . though why that nice man didn't fall in love with you instead of that one, I don't know. He must have had no discrimination at all, but at least now you're not baby-sitting night after night while Lisa gadded. Don't look at me like that, Christie, because I can't pretend I even remotely liked Lisa. I know you still have this fondness for her, and a good thing too, or you'd never have stood for her selfishness all these years. I know you miss the children horribly, but you've got a chance at last to live your own life. I do hope there's a crowd of young people on this tour.'

Janice's hopes had been dashed when she saw Christabel off. They were mainly overseas folk taking advantage of retirement to see the world, with a few people of the same age from around London. There wasn't even anyone sitting beside Christabel. Janice scowled at the vacant seat.

Christabel didn't. 'A cancellation, I suppose. It'll be heavenly. No one yapping madly in my ear when I'm on the track of some elusive way to describe what I'm seeing. It's maddening at times. I jot madly as I go, so I'll just tell people, if they ask, I'm keeping a detailed diary. Now, off you get, Janice, and don't forget, if there's any mail from Lisa, send it on to those addresses. I'm beginning to worry at not hearing for so long. I've written twice since her last. Bye-bye, I'll drop cards to you as we go.'

The coach moved off on the Great West Road, its first stopping-place Dorset. Christabel gave herself up to the sheer enchantment of the English countryside.

At Plymouth, days later, a belated tourist joined them. By now everyone knew everyone else and it had been a very harmonious tour. They were just leaving the coach to walk along the Hoe when the new passenger arrived. Gus, the courier, brought him along and said, with a beam indicating that he had brought a prize rabbit out of the hat especially for Christabel, 'I'll introduce you first, seeing you'll be sitting together, and you can make him known to the others as we go, Miss Windsor. This is Mr Tod Hurst. Now, along to the Hoe to see Drake.'

Mr Tod Hurst had a distinctly Scandinavian look about him, Christabel thought—very broad, very blond, with a hint of copper, and the bluest of eyes. His luggage had been left at the hotel they were staying at that night, he said. 'So don't let me hold you up,' and he fell into step with Christabel.

It was her first visit to this historic town and it fired her imagination—the sweep of the headlands, the magnificent curve of the shore, and, best of all, on the long promenade, the most vital compelling figure in bronze, Drake. It just couldn't be anything else but Drake. The man beside her halted as she did, as if homage was instantly demanded. He said, in a voice that held a trace of accent, 'I like it. I like it very much. The fact that there's no long text setting out his exploits . . . just that one name carved there: *Drake*. It needs nothing more than that. Drake was so much the personification of England, so much *to* England, that everybody knows. Look at him . . . his jutting beard, his stance . . . sheer confidence. He looks ready to take on the whole Armada single-handed!'

In his enthusiasm he swung round and looked at her. His eyes, she thought, dared her to laugh at his boyish enthusiasm. She met that look steadily, said, 'It makes me, at this very moment, believe completely in the legend of Drake's Drum.'

'You mean?'

'I mean that looking at this statue, one could easily believe that if England was in need, the echoes would waken again.'

He looked surprised, and she felt a faint stirring of resentment. Who does he think he is? The only one to feel moved by imaginative art?

But he nodded, 'Yes, that puts it very well.' He added, half to himself, ' "For where are the galleons of Spain?" '

Quite suddenly Christabel felt a tingling in her fingers. Such an odd thing, that inspiration for writing, which was of the mind and spirit, could be heralded, as it often was, with a physical sensation, a sort of itch to feel typewriter keys beneath one's fingertips. But this sensation was more vivid than any she had known before.

Their dialogue had been quite unheard by any of the rest of the crowd, whose chatter had drowned it out.

It wasn't till late that night, shut into the privacy of her hotel bedroom, that the inspiration became a jotting. 'Have a hero,' she wrote, 'who, in a prosaic modern world, *believes* in things.' She could make that the basis of her third novel. Her second was already started. How odd . . . you looked for a setting to inspire you, and instead, unsought, it came to you in the words of a stranger met some ten minutes earlier!

In the magic days that succeeded, inspiration wasn't fleeting or once-in-a-blue-moon; Christabel found many more as they travelled through some of the most enchanting villages in the world, rich with history and still unspoiled; coastlines were shaped tenderly with golden sands and emerald turf sloping back from the English Channel, or carved by wild weather and the roaring Atlantic into wild and fantastic shapes, each inch of shore associated with legends of the sea, smuggling, invasion, privateering. The roads, deep-hedged as they had sunk through the centuries, and winding, followed so often the old pilgrim ways to Canterbury, long distant towards the east.

On their third morning Tod Hurst said to her, 'You're an incurable jotter, aren't you? Are you writing a travel book or something? Doing publicity for a brochure?'

She laughed and said no. (True enough, it wasn't a travel book or a brochure.) 'I've been in the habit of taking notes, that's all. My father trained me in that. He became a freelance journalist—did regular column work for a couple of papers, but wasn't exactly on the staff— and if we took notes as we travelled he found it very useful. We used to compare at the end of the day. I notice you're taking some too . . . for your diary?'

He nodded, 'One forgets so soon. Not that trip books are any good to me, all divided into days. I find some days demand two or three pages, others just a line or two, depending on what you're interested in. So I take rough notes and enter them in a duplicate book at night, tearing out the top copy to send home to my people.' He grinned. 'I took screeds of notes when I was in Russia and other Communist countries, and it made it most interesting crossing the borders. They were very thoroughly examined, believe me!'

He hesitated, then said, 'I can't believe my incredible luck in getting you as my seat-mate on this trip. Imagine if I'd got that Mrs Mellaby, she'd have ear-bashed me all the way so that I'd have missed half the places of interest en route, while she either told me the entire story of her life, or tried to worm mine out of me!'

Christabel chuckled. 'Twice she came and occupied this seat before you turned up, in case I was lonely. Kind enough, I suppose, but before long she realised I was a self-sufficient creature not in the slightest dependent upon other people for my enjoyment.'

He looked at her keenly. 'And aren't you? I mean, don't you feel the need of other folk about you?'

She considered that. 'I like people, but not all the time. I'm never bored on my own. Since my father died I've had moments of great yearning to be able to tell him things, but he taught me not to keep looking back. I noticed you had a hard time dodging Mrs Mellaby.'

'Yes, she started with the inevitable: "Where do you come from?" of course. When I said New Zealand she said, "Ah, one of the big rugged sheep-farmers, I suppose?" She'd been reading an article that said there are eighteen sheep to every man, woman, and child in New Zealand and thought that said it all. I resisted the temptation to say I was brought up on a sheep station with eight thousand sheep milling about us, and confessed instead to living in Auckland, with half a million population, and twenty miles or so of city running north and south. A real city slicker. Incidentally, *you've* never asked me about myself. Not curious, or what? My accent usually triggers things off, of course.'

She laughed. 'I didn't have to ask where you came from—I recognised it for a New Zealand accent. It's very similar to my brother-in-law's. He *is* a high-country station owner. Quite near the highest peak of all ... you'll guess, near Mount Cook. He married my half-sister. The homestead is back in from Lake Pukaki. Magnificent country, I believe, though isolated.'

'How did your sister take the change from London? I take it she too lived in London?'

'Yes ... well, she has her children with her, a boy and a girl. She was widowed young and married this New Zealander who came over here. She was in a Commonwealth office and he was here in some capacity for six months.'

'You'll be visiting her some time, I suppose?'

'I hardly think so. It's expensive, travelling so far, and I'd rather put what little money my father left me into a car.'

'Wouldn't the estate stand your fare if your sister wanted you for a visit?'

She looked at him in surprise. 'I like to be independent, thanks. I wouldn't take money from her in-laws. If ever I have enough money of my own, I'll go like a shot, but only for a time. I'm a great believer in husband and wife being on their own. I've done quite a bit of travelling with my parents on the Continent, but that's so near.' She looked out of the window at the sea. 'Just a hop, step and jump from Britain.'

He nodded. 'Yes. Back home we take a crossing like the Channel one even to get from the North Island to the South Island. And leagues of ocean stretch between us and Australia, though of course, by now, air travel has shrunk the world. In fifteen or sixteen hours we can be in Los Angeles from Auckland. So different from what it used to be. When our early forebears left the Northern Hemisphere to seek a new life in a young country, they knew that in all probability they'd never see their sisters and brothers again, their parents—couldn't afford to. In the main they started from bedrock. And when I say bedrock, I mean just that.

'They were granted land as long as they could stock it by a certain time ... the biggest grants were farthest from civilisation, so they pushed on into the wilderness, fording terrifying rivers ... nothing like the gentle streams here ... where there were no roads to follow. For instance, across the Canterbury Plains, from the mile-wide Rakaia River to the Ashburton, a treeless, waterless plain, there was just one sod turned in the everlasting tussock to guide the drays and covered wagons. Sometimes they reached their granted holdings and found it devoid of trees they could fell and saw across pits for timber to build themselves a house, so they lived under canvas in tearing winds, in hail and rain and snow or scorching heat and dust-storms, till they could turn the sods to build walls of those ... thick they were, and snug once they were built. Draught-proof, primitive, unlovely till they planted trees and creepers about them.

'But in these days, when magnificent roads come within a few miles of even the most remote holdings, when even the distant ones have air-strips for emergencies and crop-dusting by plane, telephones, television ... there are those who come out and call it primitive! Who only saw the wool cheques before they came, the lamb cheques, and don't want to share in the hard graft that's still needed to keep producing!'

Christabel blinked. He sounded quite bitter. Odd that a city man should take this so much to heart, almost as if it mattered to him personally. But of course he had spoken of a farming childhood.

He saw the look, said, 'I sound as if I've a chip on my shoulder. Sorry. It's just that recently I've come up against an attitude like that, in the last few months I was in New Zealand. It threatens to destroy a marriage, a whole saga of family life if you like, spent on one property. Not all newcomers are like that. We get many we value, who love the place, who still know homesickness, but conquer it. And England and English people have been very kind to me.' He changed the subject. 'I can't believe that tonight we'll be at Tintagel. How incredible! I was brought up on tales of the Round Table. My mother was a romantic, so was Dad, come to that—they still are. They were great story-tellers.'

'So were mine,' said Christabel. 'Specially Dad. They'd both been married before, so they weren't young when they had me. They could have been too set in their ways to bother much with a small child, but I always felt Dad enjoyed my story-time as much as I did. Do your parents live in Auckland too?'

'No, in the South Island. But I go down frequently, and they often fly up for a month or two.'

They turned back to their silent contemplation of the Cornish countryside, listened to the occasional voice of the courier recounting history and legend. It was nearly night when they came into Tintagel where they would spend all the next day. . . .

It couldn't have been a fairer day. The sea was as blue as any round the coasts of New Zealand, Tod said, in a January summer there. Christabel, tossing back the shoulder-length golden-brown hair from her ears, said, laughing, 'As any round the Mediterranean, grotto-blue with shining white foam frilling the edges.'

They had dropped a little behind the others, their own booklets in their hands. The courier, with an indulgent smile, said to the others, 'They don't really need us.' Tod's blue eyes met her greenish ones and Christabel pulled a face. 'I hope he means only, because we know a fair bit about it already.'

The sea-blue eyes glinted. 'You mean rather than think we obviously like to be by ourselves. But he could be right on both counts.'

She achieved a shrug. 'We're the only two of the younger generation, so it's natural. It doesn't mean a thing.'

He lifted a bleached eyebrow. 'Who says so?'

'I do. You'd better be warned, Mr Tod Hurst. There's a parallel in shipboard romances. I recognise it for what it is—fleeting. So if you take on any more coach tours, beware.'

'I'm not taking any more.'

'That sounds very decided,' she commented.

'It is. This is the one and only.'

'Why did you take this, then?'

His lips twitched. 'I had a very special reason and I've been most agreeably surprised and impressed.'

'Then why so emphatic you'll never take another?'

'Because this for me, because of that special reason, is unique. No, I shan't tell you why—yet—however much you tease!'

'Then I shall stop asking. Isn't it the most glorious day? Oh, from this map, we're just descending into the Vale of Avalon. How fitting that there isn't a breath of wind. Not even the grasses are stirring.'

He took her elbow, said softly, 'I think we could re-member King Arthur here, even if no one can be sure this *was* his stronghold, though from these walls, and its mag-nificent position, I'm sure it was his. But certainly we can remember Tennyson. It must have been on such a day as this that he came here, sat on this turf, composed those immortal lines . . . I'm sure you know them, Christabel,

"... If indeed I go ... to the island-valley of Avilion
    Where falls not hail, or rain, or any snow,
    Nor ever wind blows loudly, but it lies
    Deep-meadowed, happy, fair with orchard lawns

And bowery hollows crown'd with summer sea
Where I will heal me of my grievous wound." '

Magic stirred in Christabel's veins. What sheer perfection! She had thought never to find again anyone as kindred in poetry, in his love of places, as her father. But she had.

On the heels of that moment a stabbing sensation of loss succeeded. This man was just a tourist. He would be leaving England soon, going thirteen thousand miles away. She tore her mind away from the realisation of how unwelcome that thought was. Hadn't she just said, laughingly, that an association like theirs was equal to the impermanence of a shipboard romance? How stupid and how vulnerable could one be?

But later that night she was to wonder if all such things *must* be fleeting, if sometimes it wasn't *merely* the passing spell of tropical nights in mid-ocean, under potent moons? If sometimes shipboard romances weren't all gossamer and rainbows, if sometimes they lasted? And if they could be real, then why not this, too?

Tod Hurst took her walking along the quaint village street, past the old stone post office that had once been a manor house and was beautifully preserved, away from the little houses, with their air of a dreaming and richly eventful past, out on to the lonely cliff-tops, where now on the late summer night the faintest of zephyrs stirred at their temples.

'Perhaps it's the Gulf Stream making it so mild,' he suggested. 'Perhaps that's a breeze that came along with it, all the way from the Caribbean, giving us a tang of spicy shores on faraway islands. Or is my geography all wrong? But what matter? . . . anything is possible here in this enchanted place.'

She laughed at the fancy, but, 'I'll go along with that, Tod.'

He said, 'Everyone warned me how unpredictable English summers are, but England's turned on the best summer for years for me, so far. I wonder if it'll last.'

'They predict it will. You ought to change your mind and fit in another tour before you go back—say the Lake District and Scotland. Given good weather, that's magnificent. The Wordsworth country, then the Trossachs, the Highlands, the Borders. That's the ideal time, autumn, for Scotland.'

'If I did, in between the business I must attend to, and departure time, would you book on the same tour?'

Her 'Why?' was out before she could check it.

He said, rather deliberately, 'It could be to get to know each other better.'

With all her heart she longed to assent. What then made her hesitate? She didn't know. It was just as if she felt some pit yawned before her and she dared not take another step.

She said, a little breathlessly, 'No ... at least I don't think so. No, I *know* I mustn't do it. I've work to do.'

'Didn't you tell me you took in typing?' he queried. 'Need you be tied to a rigid timetable? Can't you please yourself what you take and when you do it? Or if you have some with a deadline, could you cope with it in, say, two or three weeks, and book a trip for after that?'

Christabel had to school herself to refuse. What future would it have, getting involved with someone from so far away? He let it go.

They walked on, came to some gnarled old trees on the cliff edge. The moonlight silvered the leaves, shone in a radiance of light upon the dark sea below, making a moon track that seemed as if it could lead to another world.

Tod said, 'On such a night as this, both King Arthur and Tennyson could have walked here. And now us.'

They paused. He turned her round to him. He sensed her reluctance and the bright moonlight revealed to her that the corners of his lips were turning upwards. The smile was in his eyes and his voice too. 'I know it's been just a little while. We've both been cagey, a little distrustful of being thrust into each other's company. But I think we ought to give ourselves the chance of getting to know each other more. May I visit you in London? If you won't come on another tour, I'll stay in London for the rest of my time in Britain. I just don't want to let you go out of my life in three days' time, Christabel. I won't say any more just now ... I can see you don't want to be rushed off your feet.'

Illogically then she wanted to meet him halfway, to say yes, she'd book on another trip. But again that strange feeling swept over her, like a warning. As if this man was strange, too reticent about his life in Auckland. She said, 'I'll give you my address and phone number, but if, after you've had time to think, and this holiday mood has subsided, you don't want to ring, I shan't be hurt.'

He laughed, with a note of teasing merriment in it. 'Oh, Lady Caution! But I like it. You aren't a bit like—like some women. You wouldn't be hurt, you say? But would you be *disappointed*? Tell me honestly?'

Christabel hesitated, thinking, then said very seriously, 'Yes, I'd be disappointed. I've liked being with you. But you don't have to follow this up.'

Again that infectious chuckle. 'Oh, Christabel! You sound so sedate, so sensible, and I'm sure you aren't really that way. I think you're warm flesh and blood ... and would enjoy this....'

He gathered her close to him, shifted his feet to bring them into closer bodily contact, bent his head, his lips touched her cheek, cool beneath his warm lips, then he moved his mouth to hers and found the answering warmth he had looked for.

When, finally, he released her, he said with a brief but possibly exultant laugh, 'I'll follow it up all right! And who knows, a few more moments like that and I might be able to persuade you to show me Scotland in the autumn after all.'

She said, and was surprised to hear her words were shaky because that kiss had been quite a revelation to her ... never before had she known such a response within her to a kiss ... 'I think we'll make our way back to the hotel, Tod. We start early and I've got some writing to do. I must finish it.'

He laughed. 'Great excuse, letters to write. But all right, we'll stroll gently back. That will do to be going on with.'

She said, making conversation, 'And no matter how late we retire on this trip, I still like to read an hour or two.' She laughed. 'Though I was really foolish last night, didn't put out my light till three.'

'Heavens . . . some engrossing romance?'

'Not this time—a thriller. Oddly enough, although most of it took place in Europe, it finished up in New Zealand. One or two of the places I've heard my sister mention. Her husband took her all over the West Coast. This finished up there, at the Franz Josef Glacier.'

Tod said, his voice sounding oddly surprised, she thought, 'Did it really? What was it called? I'd like to read it.'

'It was *Traitor's Coast* by one Thaddeus Brockenhurst. Did you ever hear such a name? Obviously a nom-de-plume. Surely no mother would dream of calling an innocent baby Thaddeus? And I'm always suspicious of surnames the same as places. I suppose this author passed through the New Forest and called himself Brockenhurst because of it.'

'I don't agree. I've heard of quite a few Thaddeuses.' He thought of something. 'How daft can you get? If *you* wrote a book and signed it Christabel Windsor, anyone thinking on the same lines would think you'd gone to see Windsor Castle and village. Especially with Christabel being such an old-fashioned name . . . a darling, old-fashioned name. I like saying it.'

She smiled to herself in the darkness. How surprised he'd be if some day he saw exactly that name on a book cover! If their friendship continued, of course, she would tell him. She didn't linger at the door of their hotel, just said goodnight and went upstairs.

She didn't do her writing after all. It hadn't been letters, just a re-write of one incident in her book, that her publisher had requested. She had been in too happy and tranquil a mood to cope with that particular piece. Instead she set her travelling alarm clock for very early.

Just as she drifted off into a dreamy sleep she was visited by an unbidden thought: what if she too found herself living in New Zealand some day? How thrilled Davina and Hughie would be. Lisa too, really. She became aware of the trend of her imaginings and told herself not to be so romantic, so . . . so silly! He might never ring her, never call.

Her alarm rang, she rose, dashed cold water over each wrist and her face, to banish sleep, kept her gaze resolutely from the window and the enchanted world outside, and turned the eyes of her mind inward to that turmoil of spirit within the character she had created. Last night, in the aftermath of Tod's kiss, hadn't been the right atmosphere in which to write of a girl struggling against a consuming passion for a married man. But now, with a night of sleep having divorced her bemused mind from that moonlit walk, she would think herself into the loneliness of that girl's grim surroundings . . . that empty flat, peopled with the ghosts of those she had loved dearly not so long ago, and dwell with her on the promise of a delightful comradeship, if she took that one step from which there would be no return. If only, if only, he had been free. . . .

She became, as always, completely absorbed, her ballpoint flying across the pages of the pad Janice had stuffed into her bag at the last moment, when she had left from her place and discovered she had forgotten the most important thing of all.

She read it over, was gratified to find it now sounded much more authentic, and tucked the pad into her bag. When she got home she'd type it and return it to her publisher. It was a weak spot strengthened. Well, time for a shower and to come back to being Christabel Windsor, on the verge of falling in love, instead of a woman undergoing indecision and temptation.

Breakfast and the laughter of the crowd dispelled all that. They were setting off for Clovelly. The next two days passed as in a dream ... a magic dream of steep cobbled streets, fishing-boats bobbing on a full tide, quaint cottages, with bright flowers in miniature flower-beds, forest, and seascape and dipping hills, Every moment Christabel knew Tod Hurst was more and more kindred. She asked him no questions about his life in New Zealand. It was enough to be with him. They had plenty of time ahead to ask, to find out. He asked her no questions either. It was as if they wanted to accept this interlude uncluttered by the past. Christabel thought it was an ideal way to meet someone who was going to be import-ant in one's life ... away from individual settings. So that personality stood out, not submerged into a background.

They came to Lynmouth down the steepest hill of all, forested on either side, plunging as the torrent plunged till it lost itself out at sea. The light was golden, the air clear. After dinner, once more they walked, exploring the narrow streets, leaning on the bridge watching the dip-ping and soaring flight of the swallows above the waters, after insects. Christabel was glad ... or so she told herself, that he did not kiss her goodnight. They talked instead of how they both loved London. Tod said that his boyhood and manhood reading seemed to meet in this, his first pilgrimage to the city he had known so well through printed pages and fine illustrations.

'Will you come with me, Christabel, to see the places I've not seen yet, or revisit the ones I've loved best? ... Carlyle's house in Chelsea, Johnson's house in Gough Square, wander up Fleet Street with me ... what a magic word! I'd like to spend more time in St Bride's in that street ... It seemed wonderful to me that when they were restoring it after its disastrous bombing in 1940 in the true tradition of giving beauty for ashes, they should uncover all those earlier churches, until they'd revealed nearly two thousand years of worship and burials. You will come with me, won't you?

'And we'll go out again to Stoke Poges ... I suppose you've often been there, but you must be with me this time. I was fascinated to find it so unspoiled, that you could still see the cattle winding slowly homeward o'er the lea. To walk with you beside the Thames and stand on Westminster Bridge, very early one morning, and think of Wordsworth writing:

> "This city now doth, like a garment, wear
> The beauty of the morning——"

He paused.

Christabel said dreamily, finishing it for him,

> ' "Dear God! the very houses seem asleep;
> And all that mighty heart is lying still." '

He said, 'So you will do all those things with me? We're so much one in those things, aren't we?'

She didn't reply. Warning bells kept ringing in her mind. He was by no means an introvert . . . quite the opposite . . . he was an articulate man, could express himself better than most men of his age, was completely uninhibited about quoting poetry, to her, or even to others in the party on occasion, but he gave nothing away of his life in New Zealand. Her father had urged her to be discriminating.

He said suddenly, when her silence grew too long, 'Christabel, is there someone in London who would object to my monopolising your time? Some man, I mean?'

She turned her appealingly concave face up towards him in the fading twilight. 'No, but I did say I was going to be very busy, didn't I?'

'Too busy? Do you have to be? Because my time here is so short now. Will you spare as much time as you can?'

'Ring me after a week or so. That should give me time to catch up on my work. More than that I can't say.'

Tod scowled horribly, then his face cleared, and he laughed. 'All right, you cagey girl! Maybe you'll be more sure of me in London, so I'll make myself content with that.'

It would be six weeks, no longer. Long enough to find out more, she supposed. But if she saw too much of him, life was going to be very empty when he took off again, soaring up into the sky at Heathrow, going out of her life, possibly for ever.

She was a little more sure of her own feelings as they neared the end of the junketing. They had shared the holiness of Glastonbury, the awesomeness of Stonehenge, and came to their last night, at Winchester, the ancient capital.

They went for a long walk together . . . it was a perfect English evening of late summer. The scent of roses and lavender hung heavily on the still air, the birds seemed loth to cease their songs of rapture, and the crickets' dry chirruping added a drowsy sound of sheer contentment. They sketched a salute to the statue of King Alfred as they passed, laughing a little at their own absurdity, 'But he deserves it,' said Christabel. Finally they climbed up St Catherine's Hill in the moonlight. They found a seat and sat down, gazing out over the lighted ancient city below them, content for a long time to just share the silence.

Then Tod turned to her and as she looked up she caught the fair glitter of his hair in the light of stars and moon. She laughed mischievously, 'You look so Scandinavian tonight I can imagine you as one of the invaders King Alfred fought so bravely and so fiercely. Is it Nordic ancestry that makes you so fair?'

'It is, Christabel. I'll tell you all about it some time. But tonight is our last night on this trip. I'd like to hear about *you*. Till now it's been a case of getting to know each other as we are. Now I feel we ought to fit in the missing pieces of the background to the jigsaw. Tell me about you, and I'll fill you in on my background, my job, my home folk, when I come to see you in London. It would take too long tonight.'

She told him of her parents' late-in-life marriage, of having a half-sister much older than herself, the one living in New Zealand. She didn't mention her coming novel; one book didn't make an author. She was far too shy to tell everyone of her first acceptance. Wait till she was established. She said nothing of Lisa's selfishness, only that she missed Davina and Hughie very much, as when Lisa had been widowed, naturally, she had helped bring them up. There'd be time to confide more, if Tod came to see her in London.

Suddenly she said crisply, 'That moon has sailed a long way across that sea of clouds. We must go back. It's an early start tomorrow, and a lot to see on the way.'

He rose, drawing her with him, slipped his arms about her. 'Let's say goodnight here. Our communal hotel isn't exactly consistent with romance—no privacy. I've a lot to tell you, soon, Christabel, and I'm afraid some of it isn't good hearing. But don't let the thought of that rob us of any of the sweetness of this moment. I like a woman in a white dress on a summer evening in England. I like the tan of your arms and throat against that white. I like the line of your cheek and jaw, Christabel, and the way you walk and the way your laugh lilts . . . and your name and that little groove in your chin . . .' He kissed it, lingeringly, and came to her lips.

Suddenly, after gentleness, he was more urgent, more demanding. 'You like me a little, don't you? I mean more than a little? Enough to bear with me when I tell you some things you won't like? And forgive me?'

To his surprise she pushed him away, looked up at him searchingly. 'What can you mean? Oh, that's stupid. It's late and you said you'd rather tell me in London. You must have a good reason for that. And although I've had doubts about your reticence about your life in New Zealand all along, tonight I'm—I'm inclined to trust you.'

She was caught against him, kissed passionately, and found herself returning kiss for kiss. Then they stood for some time, not kissing, but still holding each other. Finally Tod said, 'That moon is aiming for that bank of cloud. I don't want you spraining your ankle in the dark. I must get you down. After all, we have plenty of time ahead of us.'

In which he was quite, quite wrong.

CHAPTER TWO

BREAKFAST next morning was a hurried affair. They were due in London early afternoon and there were two or three historic places to visit en route. Christabel was at the table before Tod arrived down, and because she hadn't finished her packing, excused herself almost immediately and went back upstairs. Their eyes had met in mutual remembrance, very fleetingly, that was all.

She still felt dreamy and bemused after last night, so found it hard to keep her mind on the packing, and twice she unlocked her case to put in forgotten items. Nevertheless she was in her seat before Tod was. The driver sounded the horn twice before he appeared.

Christabel immediately noticed he had gone very pale. She said, in a concerned voice as he took his seat beside her, 'Tod, are you all right? You look quite different from the way you looked at breakfast. What is it?'

He managed a weak grin. 'I'm all right. Just a bit heady, that's all. I didn't sleep well, which is unusual for me. I'll be fine.'

He certainly didn't look as if he would be, but she realised too much fussing would irritate him. She said in a low voice, 'Would you like that window beside you open? Perhaps lie back for a while and close your eyes? We don't have to talk madly all the way.'

He nodded. 'Suits me. Thanks.'

He kept his eyes closed, but she was sure he wasn't sleeping. A deep line had grooved itself between his brows, and there were lines of tension ... or was she being fanciful? ... about his well-cut mouth. She kept quiet, looked out on the gentle scenery and just glanced at him from time to time. He opened his eyes when they stopped at Alton for a quick visit to a church where, in the cruel days of the Civil War, the Cavaliers had made a last stand within the church and had shot it out above their dead horses, within the holy building itself.

In answer to her enquiry he said, 'No, I won't come in, thanks, I'll take a short walk in the fresh air.'

'Would you like me to come with you?'

His brows contracted immediately, so she said quickly, 'I can see absolute quietness is what you need. Pity everyone's chattering so much this morning. I think they're excited about going home and making the most of new acquaintance . . . they've thought of all they ought to tell each other about themselves.'

Tod nodded. 'And perhaps it's better than being too reticent.'

What an odd thing to say, Christabel thought as she followed the others through the bullet-studded doors. He had such an odd look—more disturbed in his mind than ill. She thought back to last night. He had asked her about herself, then told her he had things to tell her she mightn't like. What did that add up to? Perhaps at some time in his life he had rather lived it up and thought he should make a clean breast of that, but now, realising he had committed himself, thought he had been rash. That would be it. When he did come clean, she must be very understanding. She felt less worried about him now.

For the rest of the trip he did doze, heavily, exhaustedly. How strange! Now Christabel felt flat. What an anti-climax! Once they reached Windsor the miles seemed to melt. She willed him to wake up, to seem refreshed, to be more as he had been during the whole trip, a dear companion, with kindred interests.

At Colnbrook he seemed to revive a little, enough to inspect the courtyard of the both famous and infamous inn, the Ostrich, where in distant ages guests going to Windsor Castle used to stop to tidy themselves and robe before going into the presence of the royalty of the day; where Dick Turpin leapt from his window on to his waiting horse, when Bow Street Runners had almost caught up with him; where probably the Black Prince returning from the war with France, with a royal prisoner in his captive train, met his father, Edward the Third.

Christabel's spirits rose ... Tod even took a note or two. But apart from a comment on the gruesome history of the bedroom with the trapdoor where unsuspecting travellers met their doom in the time of Henry the First, he said little, and as soon as they were mobile again, silence sat heavily upon him. Christabel stared out at the traffic of the Great West Road and couldn't believe this was happening to her. Something was wrong.

As her flat was in St John's Wood and Tod was staying at Hampstead in a boarding-house, she thought he might suggest they share a taxi, but he didn't. She made one attempt, said, 'Tod, a taxi is easiest for me. Would you like it to take you on?'

He took his head. 'Thanks, but no. I'm calling at my bank for mail. The boarding-house kept my luggage for me during all my trips, but my mail still goes to my bank. It's close by Piccadilly. From there the tube is easier.'

As they picked up their bags he said suddenly, 'Heavens, I nearly forgot. You know I was last out this morning? You'd left something in your room. The house-maid asked me to give it to you. Here you are. It is yours, isn't it?' He still had that strange look on his face. He fished a pad out of his overnight satchel.

Christabel took a brief look at it, said, 'Yes, it's mine. Oh, I see what you mean. It's got another name on it. I spent the night with a friend before leaving and she gave me one of hers. I'd forgotten mine.'

Then, with a suddenness that left her staring after him, he said, 'Well, goodbye,' and walked out of the coach terminal.

Not: 'Then I'll see you in a day or two,' or, 'Goodbye till I ring you,' ... just nothing. Finish. Something inside Christabel froze. She managed to call out a careless-sounding, ' 'Bye, Tod ... nice to have known you,' and hoped he'd think from that that she too felt their acquaintanceship should end there.

How glad she was that Janice was away for a few days. If she had come round, eager to hear all about the tour, Christabel felt she just might have been unable to put on a show of having enjoyed every moment. As she had ... till the time Tod had entered the coach this morning. Her brain milled round the problem for hours and always came up with the same answer: he simply didn't want to take it any farther. How humiliating for him to make that plain, when she'd been the one to hint to him that holiday contacts were not meant to be taken seriously!

By next morning she was telling herself that there was always work. Here she was, twenty five, with her own nice flat, about to have her first novel published in a few months' time, her second one well on the way in the rough copy. And she must type out now that alteration her publisher wanted, that she'd scribbled out that night on tour. She wouldn't mail it in. She'd take it in, because some personal contact would be good for her, take her mind off Tod Hurst.

An inner voice said, 'What if he rings when you're out?' She answered it sternly, 'Then he can ring again. If he wants to. I'm not staying in on the offchance.' And she didn't.

A week later she knew he wasn't going to ring. A horrible week it had been, with hopes rising every time phone or doorbell rang, only to plunge into the depths again.

One night, at an unholy hour, she woke convinced Tod wasn't the sort of man to act like this. He must have felt really ill to behave that way so suddenly. What if he hadn't rung because he *couldn't* ring? He must be ill. Perhaps some frightfully serious infection had been settling in, even on the trip home. He'd been rushed to hospital, was there now, sick, alone in a country not his own!

But what could she do about it? He hadn't even given her the telephone number of that Hampstead boarding-house. That had been odd in itself, she supposed, but then he'd been going to ring her. All next day thoughts of him alone and hospitalised niggled at her. If only when he'd said he was at Hampstead, he'd mentioned the name of the boarding-house. Suddenly she had an inspiration. She could ask at the coach depot. When she had booked, they had asked her address and phone number in case of some alteration, so they would have his. She hoped she wouldn't sound as if she was chasing him up, but oh, what matter what strangers thought?

She made up a good tale. She waved a book at the clerk in the booking-office. It was a quiet time and the woman was quite willing to talk. Christabel said, 'I've done such a stupid thing—I was on Tour Twenty-one that got back here a week ago and I was sitting next to a man who lent me this book. I promised faithfully to mail it to his boarding-house . . . and I've lost the slip of paper he gave me with his name and address on. I wondered if you could supply it. I hate to lose books myself and I would like to get it to him.'

'Yes, I'll give it to you. No trouble. What was his name?'

'Mr Tod Hurst, and he was a latecomer. He got a cancellation and joined us at Plymouth.'

The woman opened a book, ran her ballpoint down the page, said 'No one here of—oh, you've got it wrong. It's not Hurst. It's Brockenhurst—T. Brockenhurst. He——' her eye fell on the book, she read the title, and burst out laughing. She said, 'For sure he'd want that back, it's his own book. Thaddeus Brockenhurst—I remember now. His publisher's secretary booked this for him and said he'd like to go as Mr Hurst. People made a fuss of him on some Continental trip and he didn't want a repeat. I can't understand it myself. If I was clever enough to write a book I'd rush round the world telling everybody I was an author, wouldn't you?'

In her shock Christabel stammered. 'I—I—well, I don't know. I suppose it c-could be awkward. You'd never know if people liked you for yourself or because you were famous. And I have heard people are always wanting to tell authors the story of their own lives and get huffy if they don't take the idea up.' Her brain was whirling.

The woman said, 'Well, fancy that now! I never thought of it that way. Anyway, she booked him as Thaddeus Brockenhurst and then rang back to say he preferred to be called Tod Hurst. Perhaps Tod is a nickname for Thaddeus. So we went along with it. But he evidently told you—I mean, lending you the book. Did you think the Thaddeus bit was his pen-name?'

Christabel shook her head. 'No, he didn't tell me it was his book. He merely lent me this when I ran out of reading.' Oh, dear, what a liar she was becoming! But in a very good cause. She thought of something and managed to giggle. 'Heavens! And I was scathing about that name—said it was obviously a made-up one suggested by Brockenhurst in the New Forest, and that in any case nobody, surely, would call an innocent little baby Thaddeus?'

The woman gazed at her in near-horror. 'Oh, my dear, you really did drop a clanger! Well, travelling incognito isn't all honey, by the sound of things.' Then she giggled. 'It'll be a yarn he'll tell against himself for years, I shouldn't wonder. Look, you'd better not let on that we let the cat out of the bag. But how, if you've got to post it back? Oh, you'll just post it to Hurst, of course, and the boarding-house will know.'

Christabel nodded. 'If you let me have the phone number, I'll just ring and tell him I've mailed it. I guess he'd tell the landlady the joke.' She was proud of her quick thinking, but glad when someone entered the office. She'd trip herself up yet.

The woman copied out the address, held it out and said, 'Does that sound like the name of the place?'

'The very same,' said Christabel untruthfully, and hurried out. She went into a tea-rooms and ordered herself a pot of tea and a crumpet. This put a different complexion on things. Was this what Tod had meant when he said he had things to tell her she mightn't like? Had he felt he shouldn't have been travelling under an assumed name? Especially when she'd made such a *faux pas*. But that was very trivial, surely? He'd know she'd just chuckle over it.

He'd get a surprise, possibly a pleasant one, when he knew she too was a writer. It meant they were more kindred than ever. She was sure now he must have been taken ill. She'd get back home and ring. He'd think she was smart to have worked out how to get his number. He'd be very glad to see her at his bedside. She had to pull up her racing thoughts. Don't be too sure, Christabel.

The first blow came when she asked to speak to Mr Brockenhurst. The voice sounded puzzled, then assured her that no one of that name was staying there. She said, 'He had an unusual first name, Thaddeus.' Another blank. She said desperately, 'Is that a boarding-house?— oh, perhaps I've the wrong number.' She repeated it. The number was correct. She tried again. 'He does call himself Tod Hurst for short—have you a Tod Hurst?'

'No, my dear, I haven't. I wouldn't blame a man for shortening a name like Thaddeus, but it's odd, isn't it?'

Christabel knew it was odd, but decided against saying where she'd met him. What was the good? He'd probably given the name of a boarding-house he'd seen somewhere. She thanked her, hung up.

Well, of all the devious men! If Tod Hurst . . . Thaddeus Brockenhurst . . . *was* ill, he could lie lonely in his hospital bed for all *she* cared! She knew there was still one avenue open to her . . . his publisher wouldn't part with his address, she knew, but would, of course, forward a letter. But she wouldn't, for the sake of her own pride, chase him up. She had a violent wish to bump into him in the street some day and tell him exactly what she thought of him. That *he'd* suggested they keep in touch, not *her*. Meanwhile, there was work.

She wouldn't go travelling in search of settings again till spring. Autumn in Scotland would be too poignant now. She'd thought they might see it together. She was glad when the six weeks were up. Now Thaddeus Brockenhurst would be back in his own country and her traitor heart wouldn't leap whenever the phone rang.

She worked clean through the autumn, and though she

entered into all Janice and Tim's joyous preparations for Christmas, and was glad to be one of their family circle at that time, there was little real joy in it for her. Lisa's letters were fewer now, too, and when one did come, it depressed Christabel for days. Every line breathed discontent. Yet the little notes the children sent, separately, revealed that they were enjoying life to the full. Dad had bought them ponies, they'd helped with the lambing and the tailing, they were rearing the orphans by hand, they'd spent a night up in one of the mountain huts with Dad and the men, the other kids on the property were a great bunch. The weather was extremely hot, but they had their own pool in the river. Hughie had learned to swim, and next winter they were going to start skiing.

She didn't tell the Stennisons anything at all about Tod—or Thaddeus—whatever he liked to call himself, and though she had avoided his books ever since, Tim and Janice gave her his latest, for Christmas. She didn't start it till she was safely back home, after staying two nights with them.

She would like to have flung it into her fire, but Tim had said he would like the loan of it when she finished it, and he would be bound to ask how she had liked it. She found it a strange experience, knowing what she did about him, to become so absorbed in it that she read right through the night.

Even though he was writing thrillers, Thaddeus still revealed, through all the adventure and mystery, a passionate love of poetry, of the enchanting settings of sea and shore, mountain and lake, that flung into vivid contrast, the stark ugliness of men who plotted and murdered and destroyed lives in other ways, with drugs and blackmail. But she finished up with her tongue in her cheek, because what did it all add up to? . . . To a man who deceived as expertly as any of his own villains! A man who could lie, and leave a girl bruised in spirit. A thought struck her. Had he been studying her? Testing out her reactions? Might she find herself in his pages some day, as a gullible, easily deceived girl? Could be. That hurt most of all. She felt consumed by rage, as if she'd been under a microscope. Why should an author do that, anyway? He ought to have enough imagination to provide himself with characters as real as any ever met. She herself had. *She* didn't need to dissect people, experiment with them. She flung the book from her, on the coverlet. It fell open at the dedication page. She picked it up again. It said:

'To my parents who taught me that:
"... Sweet are the uses of adversity,
    Which, like the toad, ugly and venomous,
    Wears yet a precious jewel in his head;
    And this our life, exempt from public haunt,
    Finds tongues in trees, books in the running brooks,
    Sermons in stones, and good in everything." '

Christabel looked down on the page through a blur of tears. Her parents, too, had taught her to love Shakespeare ... and trees and running brooks. She felt more desolate than ever. Better never to have met Thaddeus Brockenhurst than to have recognised in him the man she would have liked to spend the rest of her life with, and to find him false. Oh, to the devil with the man, life was for getting on with.

January was a time of blanketing snowstorms, and disrupted traffic. A good time for writing, for visiting friends tried and true. Christabel got through it. Lisa hadn't written for weeks, neither had the children. This was what time and distance did to you. February was bitter cold, but the snow had gone and now, in the gardens below the flat windows, crocuses were appearing, and snowdrops. The ground looked hard and cold, but sap was stirring in the trees. ... Christabel heard the plop on the carpet of the downstairs hall that indicated the mail had come.

She ran down ... oh, quite a pile for her, and one from Lisa. Easy to recognise the distinctive New Zealand envelope with the border of Maori art. She ran back up without examining it more closely, dropped the others on her desk, picked up her paper-knife to slit the envelope, then stared. The typed address hadn't alerted her that this wasn't from Lisa, as her half-sister always typed her letters. But this had a sender's address on and it said:

'Conrad Josefsen,
Thunder Ridge,
Private Bag, Mount Cook,
South Canterbury, New Zealand.'

Not even Rogan Josefsen, Lisa's husband, who might have written if she hadn't been well . . . or had sprained her wrist or something, but Conrad Josefsen, who didn't even live at Thunder Ridge. He was part-owner, sure, but preferred city life, she believed, and lived in the North Island. Christabel hadn't heard much of him, bar a passing reference in Hughie's letter last year, when evidently the uncle had been holidaying on the farm. What on earth was *he* writing to her for?

She felt strangely unwilling to go on unfolding the letter, then she told herself not to be stupid. It was a thick letter, though. How odd. Out fell the last letter she'd written Lisa, *unopened*. Christabel began to shake. She dropped the one large sheet that had been folded round it on the desk-top and began to read, hardly able to believe what her eyes were taking in.

'Dear Miss Windsor,
I'm sorry to have to return this letter of yours to your sister, but I have no means of delivering it and so thought I should return it to you. This may not, of course, surprise you, as it is on the cards your sister may have been in touch with you, but if not, the situation, briefly, is this: Your sister left her husband, my brother, three weeks ago, with some man she'd been meeting at Mount Cook. Some wealthy businessman from overseas, I believe.
She left a very callous note saying after a couple of weeks or so she would send for the children, and in time, no doubt, Rogan would get a divorce. That she

would be in touch, that she simply couldn't stand the
life here any longer and it was Rogan's own fault. If
he'd made it clearer how primitive the conditions were,
she'd never have married him. Since then, we've not
had a single word from her. My brother is very
attached to these children—in fact he's a better parent
to them than Lisa was. But at present he is gravely ill
in Timaru Hospital, having had a very bad smash in
his car, trying to intercept Lisa and this man before it
was too late.

I'm back on the farm. Fortunately my work is such
that I can take indefinite leave. The old homestead is
occupied by a retired couple, and they've been bricks.
We've moved the children over there, so they're being
well cared for. If your sister should get in touch with
you before she is with us, you must acquaint her with
the situation as regards Rogan's accident. I'm not sure
what the legal position will be. My brother is their
guardian, but everything will depend upon Lisa. She's
the children's mother, though I'm not at all sure it will
be best for their welfare to be with her in this *de facto*
relationship . . . if it lasts! My brother is in no state to
be consulted yet. He was unconscious for days and
even now seems to be in a dim world of his own.

Sorry to inflict this letter upon you, but there's no
way of wrapping it up. You're too far away to be of
any assistance, but I had to let you know. From what
the children say, they're very fond of you, so I'll keep
you informed of future developments, just as I expect
you to let me know *at once, by cable*, if you should hear
from your sister and be given her address,

                          Yours sincerely,
                          Conrad Josefsen.'

Christabel felt as if all emotion was suspended. She sat
at her desk with her head in her hands, willing her brain
to take it in, to cope with the problem. How long she sat,
she didn't know, but finally she got up, made herself some
tea, and took a biscuit with it. Then she went over the

letter, recognising that it wouldn't have been easy to write, especially to a complete stranger. It was this sort of thing her mother had always dreaded for Lisa—that her inborn selfishness would lead her to destroy something good. 'It's a fatal weakness in her, coupled with a dangerous sort of charm. How well I know it! Her own father had it. I was madly in love with him and was too young to be discriminating. I lived to rue it, but had the incomparable good fortune to meet up with your father in later life. I only hope, though, that Lisa will mature, and be less selfish. If Jamie hadn't died, their marriage would have been on the rocks.'

What a shocking thing that Lisa's second husband should now be lying helpless in a hospital in the Antipodes, while she, all unknowing, was living life up to the hilt, somewhere. Oh, Lisa, Lisa, how could you? Fancy leaving her darling children; Davina, at eleven, was old enough to realise what was happening. Hughie, who had known so many changes in his brief life, would be desolate. What agony to be so far away ... thirteen thousand miles!

The phone rang—car salesman. 'You know you told me that in spring you would like to buy a car? Well, I've got the very thing for you. One owner, a low mileage, in excellent shape. When——'

Christabel cut in, surprised to hear herself say, 'Oh, I'm sorry about this, but I won't be wanting a car now. The thing is I'm going to New Zealand. I've a sister out there, who happens to need me to look after her children. But thanks immensely ... goodbye.'

She stood staring at the instrument after she had replaced it. Had she really said that? Was she really going? Then she picked up the phone again, rang Janice, and asked her to come round.

Janice, naturally, was horrified, but said, finally, 'I don't think that either of us, fundamentally, is terrifically surprised. It was on the cards, always, that Lisa would some day make a mess of things, of other people's lives. And she has. The thing is, what are *you* going to do? What *can* you do?'

'I'm going out there, to be with the children. I can't bear to think of their state of mind as the truth dawns on them. Rogan, when he recovers, may be in no state to look after two high-spirited children. Lisa will be in touch sooner or later, when the novelty of being indulged by this wealthy fellow has worn off. He may not want to be saddled with two children he's never met. He may not even want her to have a divorce, may not want to marry her. Oh, what a mess! But if I'm there when she surfaces I may be able to beat some sense into her. Most of all, I must be there to temper the wind to those shorn lambs.

'This woman who's looking after them is probably past the age for it. It's hard on older people. I don't want my niece and nephew to feel unwanted, misunderstood. Janice, I've got to go. The money I was going to put into a car will pay for the fare—and back, if need be. Janice, don't tell me I'm mad to go.'

Janice's brown eyes were maternal as she thought of the children. 'Being you, you couldn't do anything else. If ever such a devilish situation was forced upon my children, I'd hope someone like you was at hand to help. It's always the children who suffer. Now, what can Tim and I do to help? You'll want to go right away. Thank heavens Tim's a travel agent. I'll get in touch with him right away to start the ball rolling . . . you've got an up-to-date passport, haven't you? But I think you should ring this Conrad Josefsen tonight. I believe New Zealand's about twelve hours ahead of us, depending on daylight saving or not, so if you rang about seven tonight, it'd be about seven in the morning there and that would be the best time to get him, probably.'

What a blessing friends were at times like this! It would be great to have Tim and Janice here tonight when she rang, so she would be able to turn from the phone if need be to ask Tim some travel detail, and who knew, by now the Josefsens might have heard from Lisa. She could be on her way back, if she knew about Rogan. Christabel stifled the unworthy thought that it would be most unlike

Lisa to so face the music. She was more likely to have the children sent after her, which would render Christabel powerless to help. Tim, primed by Janice, had found out the number and booked the call for her.

It came through dead on time. Christabel found her knees were shaky as she lifted the receiver. Mr Conrad Josefsen would already have been alerted that a person-to-person international call was coming to him from Miss Windsor of London.

He had been. His voice was crisp and matter-of-fact. 'Miss Windsor? You'll be ringing to see if we have any news? I'm afraid we haven't. I'm sorry to tell you that. We're afraid your sister is no longer in New Zealand. We're forced to that conclusion because my brother's accident was well reported on radio, television, the press.'

It was just as well he'd made it a long opening speech, because for a few moments Christabel would have found herself quite unable to speak. If she hadn't known otherwise she'd have thought she was speaking to Tod Hurst ... Thaddeus Brockenhurst. She felt dazed. Then she pulled herself together. It was simply another voice with a New Zealand accent.

She said, 'Mr Josefsen, I can't tell you how sorry I am about this. I'll be candid and say I know my half-sister is irresponsible for her age and very selfish, but it still seems incredible to me that she's not been in touch, even if she still doesn't know about the accident. To be out of touch with her children for so long is unforgivable.'

'It certainly is,' he said grimly.

'And how is Rogan? I liked him so much when he was here. It was too short an engagement, of course. My father wanted Lisa to leave the children with us and fly across for a visit to see her future home, but she wouldn't. How is he?'

'Not recovering as quickly as the doctor would have liked to see. It's in the spirit as much as in healing now. He's not making much of a fight. Yet he constantly asks after the children. He was on his way to being one of the best stepfathers I've ever known, had he been given time.'

'I know ... Davina and Hugh's letters have been full of the way he's played with them, read to them, taught them to ride. It really gets to me that this should have happened to him.'

His tone was harsh and grating. 'When a third person comes between husband and wife, they never think of how many lives they're about to smash up. Not till it happens.'

Christabel swallowed, said, 'I couldn't agree with you more.'

His voice altered. It didn't sound one bit like Tod Hurst's now. It was dry, rasped, sounded unbelieving. 'Couldn't you now?'

It puzzled her. Instinctively her own tone sharpened. 'Of course I couldn't! How could it be otherwise?'

'How indeed?' he said.

She gulped. 'Mr Josefsen, you don't think just because I'm a half-sister to Lisa that I could possibly condone this?'

His tone, she thought, was deliberately insulting. 'Forgive me, but I do think just that. Very often standards of behaviour run to a pattern in families.'

She strove for control, managed: 'Mr Josefsen, I realise you've had intolerable strain the past few weeks. I think this is making you feel you'd like to lash out at someone. Lisa for preference, but as she's missing, you're taking it out on me, her sole adult relative ... so I *will* forgive you. But you *must* get it into your head that *I'm* another kettle of fish. I'm only wanting to help.'

Out of the corner of her eye she saw that Janice and Tim had instinctively risen from their chairs and were regarding her with some anxiety. She shook her head at them, and her look said: I can cope!

She added. 'This is exactly what I rang for. Not only to ask how Rogan is and if you'd had any word from Lisa, but to say I'm practically on my way to look after the children. When Lisa was first widowed, I was made their guardian if anything should happen to her. I know it's different now she's married again, but with Rogan helpless, I feel someone of their own must be with them. Till we hear from Lisa. And if I'm on the spot, I may be able to reason with her when she turns up. I've got my best friend's husband with me here, a travel agent, who's already made tentative bookings for me. I'll cable you the exact flight, but I'll certainly be with you in a matter of days to assume responsibility for the children, my niece and nephew.'

She was amazed at the vehemence of the protest that was wrung from him. She felt it in the low intensity of his tone. 'Oh, *no*! You mustn't think of doing that. You'd be only one more complication in a situation that's already complicated in the most hideous way. We've got to hear from Lisa *some time* It's over to her. The children will be all right. I don't want them upset more emotionally. I can cope with them as it is. *On no account are you to come here.*'

Christabel gulped again, said, 'Then that's all there is to be said. But you have my address, Mr Josefsen, and you must allow me to give you my telephone number and if you need me for any reason, or have any news, you can ring, reversing the charges.' She gave the number in a cool, controlled voice that didn't shake, said a polite goodbye, hung up, turned to face Janice and Tim.

Then she couldn't speak. Janice and Tim moved as one, held out their hands to her. It was a joint embrace and their concern flowed about Christabel, and gave immeasurable comfort.

Tim said, 'Can you bear to fill in the gaps? We got some words of his, and of course your answers, but—oh, hell, why doesn't he want you to come?' Before she could speak he said, 'What's this about him seeming to think you'd condone Lisa's behaviour?'

The words were etched into her brain. She gave them word for word.

Janice said, 'Talk about the sins of the fathers being visited upon the children . . . *you're* suffering for your half-sister's misdeeds. I never heard anything so unjust! The man must be a fool. How many people would think like that? There's hardly ever more than one black sheep to a family. It's plain stupid, sheer bigotry!'

Christabel had a bewildered look. 'Oddly enough he doesn't give that impression. At first he sounded quite understanding and his letter was a fair enough one to be written to a stranger about her sister who'd wronged his brother so cruelly—and caused, indirectly, a ghastly accident to him. But suddenly he really lashed out. It wasn't till I said I was going out to New Zealand.'

Tim said, 'So what are you going to do, Christie? I've only made preliminary arrangements. Easy enough to wipe them.'

Christabel's eyes met his fairly and squarely. 'Oh, you can let them stand, Tim dear. Supposing the odious Conrad Josefsen boils me in oil, I'm going out to New Zealand to find out exactly how Davina and Hughie are faring.'

'Bully for you,' said Tim.

CHAPTER THREE

TIMOTHY insisted Christabel should have a two-day stop-over on the way. 'Otherwise you'll land right into the middle of a very sticky situation quite incapable, physically, of coping with it in the best way. You're not used to flying across the world and haven't any idea of how jet-lag can affect you.

'It'll be better for the children and for everyone concerned if you arrive feeling fit and not likely to get bowled out by any hostility you may meet. Normally, I'd have suggested a break at Los Angeles, but you've got this aunt in Vancouver—we liked her tremendously when she came across for your father's funeral—so how about two or three days there? Then fly to San Francisco and on to Auckland, where you'll go through Customs. You want Timaru, don't you, because you can ring the hospital there and find out how Rogan is? In that case, you'll fly on to Christchurch and take a train or coach from there. You ought to have a night in Christchurch and you must ring Conrad Josefsen from there. I don't like to think of you walking in on them at Thunder Ridge unannounced. They can't refuse to let you see the children once they know you're actually in the country.'

Even though Christabel knew a well-nigh unbearable impatience to get to the children, she recognised this for wisdom. Aunt Kit was a calm and lovely person and she couldn't help but benefit from being with her before the undoubted ordeal of gatecrashing Thunder Ridge. Even that name had ominous undertones ... perhaps it had always had a stormy history.

Now, at last, the moment she had dreaded was upon her. She was in a Christchurch hotel, in a room with a telephone, and the hotel office had booked her a person-to-person call to Mr Conrad Josefsen. She took a couple of deep breaths as she heard his voice. Nothing like having a lot of oxygen in one's lungs, when an ordeal was looming.

That voice, so reminiscent of a voice she had loved, came across the miles to her, with a note of surprise in it. 'Christabel Windsor? ... thank God you've rung! I've been trying to get you for the last week. Look, there's been some mix-up. They didn't say London calling, they said Christchurch, but——'

She cut in. 'Christchurch was right. That's where I'm ringing from. I've never gatecrashed in my life, but this I have to do. I *have* to see my niece and nephew. And if you haven't heard from Lisa, I'll take them somewhere to look after them. And ... and when she does get in touch with you again, if I think her new situation won't be in the children's best interests, I'll try to persuade her to let me look after them. I mean, this overseas business man might prefer that. Or she might want me to look after them till she gets her affairs settled—I don't know. I only know I *must see the children for myself*. I promise, though, I won't unsettle them if I'm reassured they're all right.'

She thought all the cocksureness of the tone he had used when last he had spoken to her on the telephone had gone. He sounded inexpressibly weary. His voice was heavy, flat. She felt he was seeking for words. Then, 'Miss Windsor, what are your plans? How do you intend coming to South Canterbury?'

Her heart lifted a little. He wasn't forbidding her to come.

'I thought I'd catch the express early tomorrow morning to Timaru and connect with a coach to Mount Cook. My travel agent in London, who is also a friend, and has been there, says I'd have no trouble in getting accommodation till we sort things out.'

He said crisply, 'Oh, don't be absurd! As the children's aunt you'll stay at Thunder Ridge. There's more than enough room, I assure you, and there's always been a tradition of hospitality. But I need to see you first, *and it must be away from the homestead.* There've been . . . developments. I—I can't tell you over the phone. Well, I could, but I'd prefer not to.'

'You mean you've heard from Lisa? Look, you just go ahead. I don't mind how much it costs. You *have* heard?'

'You could say that . . . in a way. But the way of it is exactly what I'd prefer to discuss in private, and face to face. I tell you what I'll do. I'll drive down to Timaru and meet you at the station. It gets in about noon. I'll check.'

'Isn't that a long way? I——'

'Not to us. About a hundred and thirty miles. It'll give me another chance of seeing Rogan. Father and Mother live in Timaru, as Lisa probably told you. They just about live at the hospital. I'll see you on the station.'

'Could we meet under the clock? I mean, not knowing each other we——'

'Oh, it's a small station. No difficulty, and I'd recognise you, anyway.'

'But I'm not in the least like Lisa,' Christabel protested. 'We had different fathers and we neither of us resembled our mother at all.'

He didn't really answer that, just said, 'It'll be no trouble. Well, that's fixed. Till noon, or thereabouts, tomorrow.'

He must have meant he'd seen photos of her. Possibly the children had shown him some. Or Lisa, though she had hardly mentioned this brother. Well, he seemed sure enough . . . serve him right if the train was packed, with dozens of girls getting off at Timaru!

To her relief and surprise she slept soundly, breakfasted early in her room, and felt reasonably equal to the coming interview. The thing that teased her mind, though, was that he had said they had heard from Lisa *in a way.* It could mean Lisa had let them know where she was, but wasn't sending for her children yet. She might even be out of New Zealand. Otherwise he would have said not to worry, they'd soon be with their mother.

She schooled herself to take a passing interest in the

countryside, and her seat-mate, a friendly student, returning to Otago University in Dunedin, helped. He told her the academic year began early in March, with holidays in May and August, and finished October or November. Schools went from the beginning of February till a week or two before Christmas, with the same breaks. The long summer vacation began then.

'Oh, you're visiting relations? Where? On the road to Mount Cook, beside Lake Pukaki ... I say, how lucky can you be? That's peak tourist terrain. I'm a climber myself, know the region well. It's a National Park. You ought to stay on and have the four seasons here. It's the only way to know a country.'

February had been a month of terrific temperatures and the plains were scorched into a tawny gold. They were intersected with huge sprawling rivers, aptly called braided rivers, winding their myriad streams through shingled river-beds, whose stones, worn smooth, had been brought down by the waters from the huge alpine chain that rimmed the westward horizon, through countless seasons of torrent and freshes.

There were gigantic paddocks, fenced with barbed wire or gorse hedges, with tall standing wheat, oats, barley, ripening towards harvest-time. Other paddocks, greener because they were well irrigated, were grazed by countless flocks of sheep with gleaming white fleeces. Not a shaggy black-faced one among them. The air was sparkling clear and the peaks stood out against a cloudless sky. Christabel's companion named some of them.

All too soon the long straight tracks began curving towards the coast and the gleaming blue of the symmetrical curve of Caroline Bay at Timaru came into view. Christabel knew a faint sick feeling in the pit of her stomach.

The student took her luggage from the rack, leapt down with it, handed it to her, bade her a friendly goodbye, got on again, and waved. Very few people were getting off, fewer still meeting the train.

Christabel stood there, tall, slim, in a simple green and

black patterned dress piped with white round the neck and armholes, a beige jacket draped over her arm, her luggage at her feet, and saw a large man in casual clothing, dark blue shirt, buff walk-shorts with matching walk-socks to his tanned knees, coming towards her. In fact bearing down on her. That was the impression. The sun shone on a very fair head.

She closed her eyes against the sudden shock. Oh, no, Fate couldn't be as cruel as that! Just when she was bracing herself to meet the hostile Conrad Josefsen, some ill-luck had brought Tod Hurst to this very platform at this identical time, the man who had stirred her heart, promised further meetings, disappeared from her ken. The half-smile she had summoned to meet Conrad Josefsen was wiped from her lips. They thinned themselves into a straight line and green lights pencilled themselves in the hazel eyes.

He'd seen her all right, and he wasn't going to pretend he hadn't. She must get rid of him before Conrad appeared. He came straight to her, said, 'Hallo, Christabel.'

She said, chin up, 'How do you do, Tod Hurst?' as formally as she could manage, 'Or should I say Mr Thaddeus Brockenhurst? Or have you any other alias you would prefer me to use?'

The blue eyes were as hard as diamonds. His tone matched hers. 'Oh, you'd better make it Conrad Josefsen here in Timaru—my first and last names. The other two were inflicted on me in between.'

For one horrible moment Christabel thought she was going to reel. He put out a hand to her. She stepped back smartly, said in an intense tone, 'Don't touch me! Just don't touch me. I've no idea what game you were playing on that tour in England, but it is the most despicable thing I've ever heard of. It's quite incredible. You must have known exactly *who I was*.'

Hardness was still in his eyes. 'I did. So I was glad I went as Tod Hurst. Tod was my nickname at school. I boarded here.'

Her lips were dry. She moistened them. 'Why? Why did

you do that? Why didn't you say when we were introduced?'

'I thought it a good chance to find out more about Lisa's background, to see if you were all the same. We were already worried about Lisa and Rogan. She appeared interested in money only, and what money can provide, not the life up here.'

Christabel was silent, digesting that. When she looked up again her eyes were pure green. 'No wonder you didn't follow up our brief acquaintance! You never meant to—you wouldn't have dared. I can't think why you took it as far as you did while we were on tour. This has certainly been a moment of revelation. If they're all like you at Thunder Ridge, the sooner I get my niece and nephew away from there the better. Now, what about Lisa?'

The strangest look crossed his face, a caring, vulnerable sort of look. She told herself, in that fleeting instant, that she must be crazy to impute that sort of feeling to this strange, hard man. He took his time to answer, then said, 'We must have a more private place than this to discuss that. I'm taking you to my parents' place.'

She flinched, visibly. 'I don't feel up to meeting any more of your family than I must, yet. You judged me as probably tarred with the same brush as Lisa . . . I feel the same about your family. They could be as devious as you. I'd rather take you on one at a time, please. Can't we go to a tea-room or something?'

'They'd be very crowded at this hour, but my parents won't be at home. They're at the hospital.'

She said swiftly, 'Is he worse? Not at——?'

'Not at danger point—recovering. The fact is he can't yet feed himself. His hands are in plaster. Mother and Dad go whenever possible; it helps the nursing staff. They won't come home till they've given us at least an hour. Mother said I was to bring you home.'

Christabel didn't know if that was ominous or not. How would any mother feel towards the sister of the woman who had been the cause of an accident like that to her son? She allowed him to take her away. They got into a huge mud-splashed estate car.

There was no flow of small talk to ease the tension. They turned into a wide paved drive that snaked uphill, a surprisingly large garden for a retired couple and an equally surprisingly large house. Seemingly Conrad Josefsen read her thoughts.

'Mother and Dad needed space about them living in the mountains so long, and as my two sisters live in the North Island and are often home in the school holidays with their families, they need lots of room.'

That was the limit of their conversation till he drew up at the pillared front entrance and took her in, through a shady hall, to a study at the back that looked out on a huge lawn equipped with swings and seesaws. A shady willow overhung the far edge and beyond that a circular clothes-line swung a row of gaily-coloured washing round and round.

Christabel stood by the table tapping her fingers on its edge nervously, gazing out at these things.

He seemed reluctant to start. She prompted him, 'About Lisa . . . you said you'd heard . . . in a way. What way?'

He pulled a deep chair forward. 'Would you sit down, Christabel?' Well, at least he'd dropped the formality of his telephone conversations.

She shook her head. 'No, I'd rather stand. I realise I'm in for a rough time and I feel I can meet it better on my feet.'

'Not this, I think—but just as you like. The reason we hadn't heard from Lisa has been explained. She and— this man—hadn't made for Christchurch's international airport as Rogan had thought but had gone through the passes to Lake Wanaka, and around the Haast Road, then up the West Coast. There was a storm and flooding.' He paused, then, 'They had an accident and they weren't discovered till . . . well, you must have been just starting out . . . I'm afraid they'd both been killed. Christabel, will you sit down, now?'

She had swayed, but not with weakness, with the impact of his words. She gripped the edge of the table,

said, 'No, thank you, I can take it. But——' she walked
swiftly over to the window, stared out at the shaven lawn,
the flapping clothes, the swaying trees, all blurred into
one.

He saw each hand come up to her eyes, rub unshed
tears away with a gesture that was curiously childish,
heard a deep breath taken, then slowly she turned round.
She had lost her colour, but she held her head high, her
shoulders square.

She said in a toneless voice, 'Then it's over to me, isn't
it? Just give me the details. I can take it. It's not my first
bereavement. If you can assist me in any way with what
may be different procedure, because it's a strange
country, I'll make all arrangements for her funeral.'

He took her arm. 'You *must* sit now. I'll give it to you
briefly, then make you some tea—or give you something
stronger. Mother left a tray all ready.'

That small gesture of sympathy from a woman whose
son's world had been turned upside down by Lisa almost
destroyed Christabel's composure. She controlled it, said,
'Tell me, then I'll settle for tea.'

He said gently, 'The funeral was the day before yesterday. We thought you could have been away from home
for an indefinite period. The car had been in the river a
long time. But if it's any comfort to you, they weren't
trapped in it. They were killed instantly when it plunged
off the bank into the swollen river.'

'Thank you, it is a comfort. And the man? What arrangements   '

'His body has been flown to England. He lived in
Hong Kong, but his only relative, a sister, lived in North-
ampton. She needn't know there was anything irregular about the trip.'

'And Rogan? How has he taken it? He's the one who
matters.'

'We can't tell. He was given sedatives at the time and
there's been no marked deterioration.'

'That's something.' Her lips felt stiff and framing the
words was purely automatic. 'And Davina and Hughie?
What have they been told? And how have they taken it?'

'How can one ever tell how children take things? We're distraught if children are too upset, worried if they appear to bottle it up. Jonsy has been very good with them, keeping them busy, letting them talk about it if they want to, then distracting them if she thinks they're going on too long. Davina has been very good with Hughie. Within herself I just don't know. She's old for her age. Sometimes I feel I'd like to see her more child-like.'

Christabel nodded. 'She's always been that way. It gets to me at times. When Jamie died—her father—she seemed to assume some responsibility towards Hughie, even towards Lisa. More than a child should.'

'Because of Lisa's nature.'

'Yes. I've got to be honest about that. She was selfish to the core . . . mostly.' Though a real sorrow was seeping through her awareness now at the thought of all Lisa's vivid beauty and charm coming to this, even death couldn't whitewash her memory. Then she said, 'How dreadful to think what I'm thinking right now . . . I never dreamed I'd ever be glad my mother and father weren't living, but I am . . . they're beyond all power of hurting. My father tried so hard with Lisa. He felt she was what she was because she'd lost her own father too early in life. I sound as if I'm trying to make excuses for her too, and I am. But the worst sorrow I feel is for the havoc she's caused in your family . . . especially in Rogan's life.' She looked up at him. 'You sound so understanding about the children, so concerned.'

He gave her look for look. 'You sound surprised. Why shouldn't I be?'

'Don't you know? Because when you spoke to me on the line from New Zealand to London, you didn't want me here because I was the same blood as Lisa . . . half the same. You thought I could be like her. You don't think that about the children. It's abominably unfair to even have entertained that thought about me. It's like something out of a Gothic novel away back in intolerant times. Like a family feud.'

He said slowly, 'It wasn't just prejudice. I had other

reasons into which I'm not prepared to go.'

Something of the unreality that possessed her left her. She stared. 'I can't think what you can mean.'

He made a gesture—of distaste, she thought. 'Of course not. Let it go. You're here and under the circumstances, for the children's sakes, perhaps it's for the best. Before this we thought their mother might, eventually, claim them, and I was far from sure it would be in their best interests. My mother was all wrought up about it. To her they're as dear as her other grandchildren and she was terrified they might not have a happy life, with this man Lisa had gone away with.'

She said, 'And now you mean I can take them away, if I like?'

'No.' She was surprised at the vehemence. 'Nothing is going to be decided till my brother recovers enough to come home. He's in no state now to make decisions, and they are his stepchildren. But it will be good for them to have someone belonging to their old life, right here. So you may stay. Now, you must have this tea. I'll bring it in.'

Christabel sank down into the chair, suddenly weak-kneed. She remained completely silent as he brought in a large tray and placed it by her easy chair. He poured her tea, didn't ask how she liked it, she noticed, so he had remembered from the days on tour ... medium strength, milk, but no sugar.

He took an assortment of things from the tray, put it on one plate, placed it on the table so she could reach it with ease. She told herself this couldn't be true ... she was sipping tea with Rogan's brother, that antagonistic man she had dreaded meeting, the unknown quantity of the international phone call, but it was Tod Hurst ... Thaddeus Brockenhurst ... Conrad Josefsen! Furthermore, he was being punctiliously hospitable to her, waiting upon her, and he was also scrupulously fair ... even if there was no doubt he would rather she was at the uttermost ends of the earth.

She blinked at her own thoughts. These islands, except

for the South Pole, *were* the uttermost ends of the earth.
To her, England—London—was the hub of the universe.
She'd been in New Zealand thirty hours and already she
was thinking of London as the uttermost end..As if this
was the norm, instead of a temporary domicile till she got
things sorted out.

She looked at the plate and found she was, after all,
hungry. Club sandwiches ... one held chicken, lettuce,
tomato; one egg, ham, cucumber; the other celery,
cheese, pineapple. No trouble had been spared. Rogan's
mother must have made those scones just before she departed for the hospital, they were so crisp, and there were
wedges of jelly sponge. Suddenly she saw them through a
blur of tears. She had to reach for her bag to get a hanky.

Conrad looked across at her and said, 'Would you like
me to go away for a bit? You might feel better if you let
go. She was, after all, your sister.'

Christabel swept the tears away with two swift move-
ments, shook her head vigorously. 'No, it's not that. I
think it's the manner of Lisa's passing, the havoc she's left
behind. I feel touched at the way your mother prepared
this ... a lunch for the sister of the woman who has
wrecked her son's life. It's so thoughtful. She'd guess I
needed something light. And it's so beautifully set out,
even to the best china.'

Conrad Josefsen was eating at the table at the window,
but put his sandwich down now, said, 'That's Mother.
She even tried her damnedest to like Lisa; devised as
many trips down here for her as possible, would ring up
the homestead and ask her down for a few days, take her
shopping and to the theatre, run her up to Christchurch
for a week or so even though she hates leaving Dad. But it
was no go. All Lisa—Oh, I'm sorry, I'll shut up.'

'No, finish it. I'd rather know.'

'Well, to be brutally frank, all Lisa was interested in
was getting as much money settled on her as possible. I
think she had some sort of escape like this in mind.'

Christabel shivered inwardly. An escape that had
proved a trap. A fatal trap.

She nodded. 'It adds up. I think it's magnificent of your mother to have reacted like this. Some people benefit greatly by the years they've lived, and can meet a situation like this.'

He nodded. 'She faced so much when we were small and ill, sometimes gravely ill. We're so remote. In those days time was always against us. Mother was like all the mountain women, she had some inner resource she seemed able to call upon. Dad pitted his strength against mountain blizzard and blanketing snow; Mother seemed to pit hers against our most dread enemy, time, when illness or accident put us at grave risk. She'd nurse us through it, then, very humanly, have a minor collapse after. But never when she was needed for the fight. It's the same now. She's single-minded about getting Rogan back to health. There are weeks, possibly months of treatment ahead, physiotherapy and so on, and Mother will pull him through. I only hope the collapse won't be too great after it.'

Suddenly Christabel felt that here was something she could help with, given the chance. She said, more crisply, 'Then it's up to us to spare her all we can—anxiety about the children, for instance, or any hint of things being difficult up at the homestead. She might be worried in case it proves too much for Mrs Johnson. What about your father?'

'He doesn't take things in his stride quite so well. All the time since Lisa came here he's suffered the pangs of disillusionment with Rogan. Perhaps because Rogan's life is bound up in the high country, and all Lisa could see in it was the value of the place. Why not sell, was her theme song from morning till night. Not that Rogan talked about it. But she tried to get at Dad about the property. And Dad and Rogan are so close. Comes from being out on the tops together so much.'

'The tops?' she queried.

'The high-tops—the mustering on the mountains. We muster on foot. It's no terrain for horses, except the little bit we have in the valleys, and the flats. We muster up to six thousand feet and more. I took on journalism and though I can take my place on the blocks with the musterers and on the stands with the shearers and love it, naturally, I wasn't there so much.

'My maternal grandfather was a newspaper editor and I took after him, though the pull of the land is so strong I sometimes feel torn between the two. You know I'm Thaddeus Brockenhurst. I worked my way through journalism to writing books. My plan now is to write them at Thunder Ridge. That is, when Rogan is well enough again to be with us, supervising, if not actually bullocking in with the men as he's always done. But I'll be able to do no more writing this year—I've made up my mind to that. The station must be kept going. It's my parents' livelihood as well as the others. And the girls have a certain income from it too. So for the time being Thaddeus Brockenhurst takes a back seat.'

That brought her back to his deception of her, to his promise to see her again. She looked at him with that green look in her eyes. 'Yes, I know you're Thaddeus Brockenhurst. That piece of chicanery is beyond me. I was so gullible. Cautious at first . . . you called me Lady Caution, remember? Then when you didn't call or ring, I suddenly thought how awful it would be if you'd been taken ill, perhaps in hospital, thousands of miles from your own kin. I went to the coach tour people, asked for your address, said I had a book to return to you and had mislaid the address. I had it with me . . . you remember I was reading it on tour? . . . your *Traitor's Coast*. The woman said, "Oh, for sure he'd want that returned to him—his own book," and gave me the address. She explained how you'd thought it better not to be known as an author on the tour, that you liked people to like you for yourself, not because you were famous. I accepted that. Ninny that I was, I still thought you might be ill. I was rueful about my clanger about your name.

'But when I rang and found no one called Tod Hurst or Thaddeus Brockenhurst had ever stayed there, I realised you'd never intended to see me again. I felt furious to think that though I'd said to you friendships on tour were like shipboard romances, not to be taken seriously, you'd behaved like that. It wasn't necessary. Now we come to something else. I've been trying to think it through. Seeing some ill-luck brought you to the same tour I was on, and because my father adopted Lisa and gave her his name—that was because her own father had a reputation for dishonesty—you must have known I was her sister, so why didn't you just say: "What a coincidence ... I believe I'm your brother-in-law-once-removed" or something?'

His voice was deliberate. He didn't sound as if he knew he was on the mat for something definitely underhand. 'Because it was no coincidence. It was a golden opportunity to find out something about my brother's wife ... find out what made her act this way. I was even ready to make excuses for her if she'd had an unfortunate childhood, been very poor, say. In the first place I meant only to call on you in London. I came to your flat and someone in the next flat heard me and volunteered the information that you were off on a Hayley's Tour. The fact that I'd been going to hire a car and drive myself round those counties influenced me, of course.'

Christabel said, between her teeth, 'And you actually planned to travel under an assumed name to find out all about Lisa's sister? What a tortuous mind you must have! I'm beginning to wonder what Lisa came to, what she——'

He held up a hand. 'It's not as cold-blooded as it sounds. After I left your flat I went to see my publisher. I asked him what these tours were like. He thought a tour was much more likely to yield gen than a solitary exploration, more human interest and all that, and got his secretary to ring Hayley's to see if they had any spare seats on one leaving soon. I didn't have a terrific lot of time left. The others were booked out, but if I liked to catch up with this one at Plymouth, there'd been a cancellation. You know the girl booked me as Thaddeus and that I shortened it to Tod Hurst. I regarded it as an irresistible chance to travel incognito with you. If it sounds poor, I can't help it. You'd probably not understand that to a writer, it was most intriguing. I felt I could use it. That is, I felt that at first.'

For some reason, the fact that she *was* a writer gave Christabel a gleeful satisfaction, that was all mixed up with justifiable fury at his perfidy.

The contempt on her face was unmistakable. 'Well, all I can hope is that if you ever do use it, you cast yourself as the villain, not the hero. You hadn't even the guts to tell me any time during that trip, or even at the end. I find that completely despicable.'

He said, 'It was—I admit that. I did say, however, that I had things to tell you, things you mightn't like about me. You can't have forgotten that.'

Christabel said slowly, considering her words, 'I'm afraid I jumped to the obvious conclusion . . . any girl would. That's why I didn't encourage you to tell me there and then. Because I distrusted—and with good reason, it seems—this sudden attraction on *your* part, for someone so newly met. I still thought it might fade when you left the tour, and if so any confessions you might make under a Hampshire moon you might regret later.'

He stared uncomprehendingly, then the penny dropped. 'Oh, you thought I was going to confess to affairs?'

'Just that.' She looked him straight in the eye.

His lips tightened. 'I suppose that's feasible . . . after all, we do live in a permissive age. You should know.'

A line creased her brow. '*I* should know? Well, yes, I live in this age. I'm part of it. My sister has just demonstrated that. I can't understand, though, what you——'

'What I'm getting at? Probably not. I'll tell you some other time. We're going to be living at very close quarters for some weeks.' He looked at his watch. 'Mother and Dad should be here soon, and I don't want them to find us in any sort of a donnybrook. They've had a tough time. It was a shock, I suppose, when I rang last night and said I was leaving early this morning to meet you off the Southerner. Are there some details you'd like to know before they arrive?'

'Yes. The funeral. Where did it take place, and how?'

'Here. Rogan had the say-so on that. When your father died, you'd mentioned to Lisa in a letter that it was a cremation service, so he assumed that's what she'd have preferred. So we had a brief service at the crematorium chapel. A minister friend of our minister at Fairlie took it, and we made it a private one. Just Mother, Father, and myself attended. We would have liked to have been in touch with you, of course, but tried and failed.'

She said, 'Don't sound so disapproving. You couldn't expect me to let you know I was coming. You would have stopped me, somehow. And I had to be with the children, even if only till we'd heard from their mother.'

'It wasn't meant to be disapproving,' he told her. 'In your shoes I'd have done exactly the same. Children need someone of their very own.'

It took away her anger and left her feeling defenceless. She was actually glad when she heard a car.

Conrad Josefsen said swiftly, 'Oh, I nearly forgot. My parents haven't the faintest idea that we've met before. They know I had a coach trip round the western counties, but not that you were on it. They'd written to Auckland before I left for Britain, and asked me to call to see you while I was there. Lisa wouldn't know, I think, because about that time she didn't see much of my parents. She spent so much of her time at the tourist village.'

'Was—that man—there a long time?' asked Christabel.

'No, but she found it gayer there, a cosmopolitan atmosphere. I just told my parents I'd called to see you, but you were away.'

'Would they have approved what you did?'

He actually had the nerve to grin. 'Hell's bells, no! They'd have both torn strips off me. There are times when they don't understand my journalistic ways. The only one who wouldn't have turned a hair was my grandfather, Thaddeus Grayson. People *do* call innocent little babies Thaddeus, after all, you know.'

She shrugged. 'I'm certainly not apologising for that. Too much of importance and tragedy has happened since.'

He said, seeming to want to make conversation, to appear ordinary when the others came in, 'He said once none of his family had ever wanted to carry on *that* name. He said it humorously, I suppose, but Mother took it seriously and thought he was a bit wistful over it. And when I had my first book accepted I suddenly thought how pleased the old boy would be if I used my middle and third names. I needed a nom-de-plume anyway, as I was in the newspaper world myself. I didn't want to appear as if I was wanting favourable reviews from fellow journalists—it can be embarrassing for friends. By now, I don't care. Just as well I am freelancing. I'll be on the station for months, if not years. We don't know what the long-term effect on Rogan will be.'

'Oh, you mustn't give up your writing entirely,' cried Christabel, stopped, surprised to hear herself uttering those words, then went on, 'I know so well how hard it is to get a start and how unfair it is to a publisher not to produce regularly when he's taken the risk of launching a new writer.'

'You do? How come?'

'Did Lisa never say? Oh, of course you didn't see much of her. Dad wrote. Nostalgic country books . . . the sort of thing you see as newspaper columns. Each separate in itself yet with a common thread running through. He'd got an early start, then force of circumstances caused him to drop it in what should have been his most prolific years. His first wife had a long illness. He couldn't run a job and nurse her at night. He picked it up in later life and made a modest success. But for someone like you— with four books behind you at this stage—it ought to be possible for you to continue even if producing more slowly.'

She became aware that two people had paused in the

doorway, and she turned her head. Somehow she had expected a buxom, cosy-looking woman. Here was someone tall, elegant, dark ... someone who said, 'Oh, you've told her you're an author, Conrad, that's good; I'm telling everyone now. It seems as if you've got on to terms already.'

'You could say that,' said Conrad Josefsen. 'I feel as if we've known each other for ages. Christabel, this is my mother and father, Kate and Ivar Josefsen.'

Christabel felt fortified by the tea and sandwiches and cakes and in control of herself again. She rose quickly, crossed to them as they came forward, held out her hands, caught a hand of each and said, 'Thank you both for having me here today. It isn't easy for you, I know, at such a time. It's rested me.'

This seemed to be the right approach. Ivar, an older edition of Conrad, cleared his throat and said, 'We were sorry you had to meet with such news when you'd come across the world to look after the children. It's very good of you.'

Kate squeezed Christabel's fingers, said, 'When we heard what you'd done we knew you couldn't be like ... I mean, we knew you must be the right sort. It will help us tremendously to know someone of their very own is looking after the children. Jonsy is wonderful, but she's getting on and is busy, anyway, always. And just now I can't be away from Timaru. I was only sorry Conrad missed you in London. It would have been much nicer for you if you could have met in a different way.'

'It would indeed,' agreed Christabel, and flickered a quick glance in Conrad's direction. 'But I'm here now and I'll hope to be able to help. How is Rogan today?'

Kate's eyes darkened. 'Physically stronger. In spirit, and mentally, I just don't know. For the first time since he was born, I can't get close to him, can't reach him at all. But then there are times in everyone's life when one has to fight things out alone. But he was glad when he heard you were arriving.' She looked across at Conrad. 'But as we were leaving, someone else came in. That could help. She flew in from Fiji yesterday. She must have been on the same flight as Christabel.'

'Barbara?' asked Conrad, his eyes alight and as blue as the sea, instead of dark with emotion as they had been most of the time.

'Barbara!' repeated Kate in a tone of utmost satisfaction. Then, as if this was something they didn't want to discuss in front of a stranger, she said to Christabel, 'You'll be tired. I think you should stay here tonight and go up to Thunder Ridge tomorrow morning.'

Christabel shook her head. 'If Conrad isn't too tired, I'd like to make it to there tonight, for Davina's and Hughie's sakes.'

CHAPTER FOUR

WHAT Christabel had dreaded was now upon her . . . being cooped up in a car for a hundred and thirty miles, with this antagonistic and deceitful man she had had the poor discrimination to fall for on that idyllic tour that seemed years ago now.

A heavy silence descended upon him and upon her. Small talk, which could have helped had he been a perfect stranger, even on a day of sudden bereavement and distressing problems, was useless. The road took them back north a few miles till, at a place called Washdyke, it turned due west.

Only then did Conrad speak. 'This is rolling country, very gentle and lush, very pastoral, as you see. Don't be deceived by it. In essence it isn't much different from parts of rural England, but beyond, the terrain alters starkly, becomes harsh and grim, with great uprearing heights, scenery carved out by terrific upheaval and gouged deeply by glacier-beds in the Ice Age. Terrifying to pit one's puny strength against and inexpressibly beautiful to *those who can take it*. This gives no idea of what lies further in.'

'Nothing can surprise me now,' said Christabel. 'I've had too recent an experience of being deceived by first impressions. Perhaps it's true of New Zealand people as well as of the land. So I'd like to state here and now that I don't consider you're in any position to adopt a holier-than-thou attitude over Lisa. She was, I admit, faithless and clandestine. What you did wasn't as appalling as that, I know, yet to me, hiding behind a nom-de-plume as you did was completely despicable. You had no justification for it.'

He said, and it mystified her, 'No . . . but I have since. I admit I was wrong——'

'That's big of you,' she broke in hotly.

He continued as if he hadn't heard, 'But I'm now convinced I was entirely wise, if not ethical.'

She made an impatient gesture. 'That's just playing with words. It comes of being an author. You can make anything sound right.'

'You're not exactly halting with your tongue yourself, I might say. Give me credit for this at least. I did try to stop you coming. You need never have known who I was.'

She glared. 'You can't have any idea what a bond exists between the children and myself. If you think I'd have weighed up the distaste of having to be at close quarters with you against their need of me, you must be incapable of understanding human emotion. What do my personal feelings matter against the fact that my niece and nephew are alone now in a strange land with all about them people who could hate them because their mother has ruined their son and brother's life?'

He stared straight ahead, then, to her surprise, said in an ordinary tone, 'You're right, of course. It couldn't have weighed against your desire to come. Even had you known.'

It took the wind out of her sails, stopped the rest of the hot words reaching her lips. He continued: 'But in one thing you're wrong. Nobody hates the children, least of all Jonsy, who adores Rogan. Mother was ill so long after he was born that, in a very real way, Rogan was Jonsy's little boy. But those children fitted in at Thunder Ridge from the moment they arrived, I was told. "Poor bairns," Jonsy called them, realising they'd had a shabby deal from life in the sort of mother bestowed upon them. It sometimes happens that selfish mothers breed unselfish children. They *have* to do things for themselves. These youngsters love the life among the mountains. They've completely identified themselves with the sheep station.

'That's another reason I didn't want an aunt coming out here and upsetting them, perhaps being disparaging about what she might think was a crudity of existence . . .

it's a basic sort of life . . . and when we knew Lisa had . . . wouldn't be coming back, I wanted you less than ever. It would be absolutely cruel to tear those children away from this life they love.'

She couldn't answer, she was too afraid her voice would break. *It was such a mess.*

Conrad's eyes left the road fleetingly, to glance at her. 'Possibly you find that hard to believe, but you'll see for yourself, and if you do have the children's best interests at heart, you'll admit it.'

She swallowed, managed to say, 'It seems Lisa couldn't take the life. So you've made up your mind I can't either. I've no idea what the future holds. I'm simply here to sum up a situation and to do, in conjunction *with Rogan*, what's best for the children. I can't see that any of the decisions rest with you.'

His voice was suave. 'At the moment they don't.' And a shiver ran through Christabel. Did he mean that if Rogan didn't recover, *his* might be the final word over the children's future? Surely not? Anguish swept over her. These people were being very fair to the children now, but if anything happened to Rogan, might their feelings change? A thick blackness descended upon her spirits.

Suddenly Conrad said, 'The worst that can happen to those children is for any sort of discord to continue under their roof. Nobody knows you and I are at loggerheads, if that's the word for it. I guess we must call a truce. I'll give you a trial. Only any hint of anything irregular in conduct, such as your sister's, among the men, single or married, on the station, and off you'll go. Understand?'

Fury rose up in her, then as quickly subsided. She must, she *must* subdue such feelings if she was going to be able to stay to look after Davina and Hughie. She said, in a tone she had reason to be proud of, 'I liked the first part of the speech. I'll ignore the last. It's too ridiculous for words. Now, don't take me up on that. I'm going to pretend you didn't say it. I'm here simply and solely to look after the children, to temper the wind to the shorn lamb. What happens to me in the doing of it simply doesn't matter.'

'What can you mean?'

'I mean whatever insults I have to suffer I must be here. I'm only too glad that you don't extend your feelings about Lisa and me to the children. I couldn't take that if you did. I'd whisk them away somehow. And your parents, bless them, haven't displayed any animosity towards me. You said a truce. When does it start?'

'Right now,' he said, and added, 'Commenting on a new landscape makes a good subject for small talk, don't you think? Or would you prefer to sit bristling with resentment in a sulky silence?'

To her everlasting credit Christabel managed a small chuckle. 'I'd find it very hard. Words usually tumble out of me. Mother used to say. "Christie never sulks . . . It'd kill her." I've been wanting to ask if these creeks we're crossing all run right into the sea.'

His interest was caught immediately. 'Why?'

'Because they're called creeks on the name-plates on the bridges, which, incidentally, I like. To have even minor streams named is a great help. In England, creeks are all inlets from the sea. But we're well inland now.'

'I didn't know that. Thanks. I've a world readership now, and as New Zealand has been called the land-of-many-waters, if I'm writing about inland areas . . . such as now, when I'm using a Lake setting, overseas readers could be quite puzzled. You must tell me any other differences you notice.'

Some of the tension eased in Christabel. Any sort of olive-branch was better than none. And looking for differences took her mind off Lisa.

Conrad said, 'Some people never notice details like that, or question them. I take it this comes from taking notes for your father. You told me that on tour.'

'Yes, it was one way I could be of assistance. Dad was too much of a giver, not single-minded enough to really succeed. Time was always against him. So if I could save some time for him, I did.'

'Time is the enemy of all writers. You don't find the time for it, you make it. I know. I wrote my first books while working full-time on a newspaper.'

Her tone was even. 'But at least your nights were your own. Dad worked full-time as a civil servant, and nursed a very sick, very brave wife at nights. The time he made was for her. Later, when he took on Mother and Lisa, he took it up again, but time ran out a little early for them both. So no one needs to sneer that my father wrote only three books in his lifetime.'

Surprisingly he said promptly, 'I'm sorry, that was insufferable of me. I'm not usually so tough. My only excuse is that I'm feeling raw.'

Christabel met generosity with generosity. 'You must be. Apart from all the personal agony over Rogan, the dreadful strain of not knowing what Lisa would do, and so on, your own life's been turned upside down, and you can't see an end to it. Added to that you've had the discovery of the bodies, and I've just realised that if you were at the funeral, you've done this return trip twice with only a short break between. And now I'm being touchy. It's just that . . . Dad was one of those unsung heroes and I miss him so much. We were such pals.

'I think our truce is very necessary, not only for the children's sakes, but for our own nerves to recover. Conrad, this scenery deserves commenting on. When does this gentle rolling country give way to the terrifying and inexpressibly beautiful stuff?'

'Beyond Fairlie. There we enter the Mackenzie Country . . . Through Burke's Pass into the mountains. This doesn't last much beyond Cave.'

'Cave?' she queried.

'The name of a township or village. Mainly known for its beautiful memorial church built to honour the principal settlers of the Mount Cook area, the first Burnetts of Mount Cook Station, which is on the opposite side of Lake Pukaki to Thunder Ridge. That's an idea,' he added. 'You ought to see the memorial church. No more vivid reminder of the early days could be shown you. If you're about to be introduced to the high-country, and are going to see it in its tamed condition, you ought to know something about it before it was bridled with hydro-electric works, and with a tar-sealed road sweeping right to its door swarming with tourists and with television aerials shining against the thunder clouds.'

It made her feel the truce was merely a surface gesture, and that underneath strong resentment still ran. What lasting harm had her half-sister done that such feeling could continue to exist? Or, to be fair, was it only the writer in Conrad that made him love dramatic utterances and contrasts?

He turned off the main road at Cave, the tiniest of villages, past darling little wooden cottages, and up a road that wound up a sizeable hill, then dipped down to a dell-like road, with a church set among trees above it.

She gazed, said, 'I know I'm all at sea with the seasons. This is late February. Is that early autumn? Back home, the early snowdrops are appearing. Yet I can see spring-like blossoms on those trees there.'

'It's really the last month of summer, but autumn comes early up here against the mountains, and those are mountain ribbonwoods. They bloom in autumn, and, though I've not realised it till now, they do give an illusion of frail spring blossom.'

They drove up. Here was St David's, the shepherds' church. It was built on the lines of English churches . . . it had a Norman tower, but it was fashioned of glacier-borne boulders from the valleys about them, boulders that had been brought down by the Ice Age, from the foremost ranges. Fitting that a place of worship should have been built from the earth beneath its feet. Conrad took her into a rough open porch first. A tablet said:

'This porch
is erected to the
Glory of God
and in memory of the
sheepmen, shepherds, bullock drovers
shearers and station hands who pioneered
the back country of this Province
Between the years 1855 and 1895.'

They came to the front door and entered into the dimness, lit by a shaft of sunlight that shone from the north, which made Christabel realise it was indeed a topsy-turvy world.

All about on the walls were tablets with Gaelic inscriptions, the old, dear language of those who had ventured such leagues of ocean and land to wrest a new living for themselves, fleeing from conditions that had been even more trying in the land which had given them birth.

The woodwork was from the forest, rough adzed pews in which no nails were used, just pegs, pews made of the Southland red beech which the early settlers had called birch because of its tiny leaves. Everything here spoke of the great forever, built to last. Not like Lisa's marriage. The floor, on an incomparably solid foundation, was of *totara* blocks, beautifully polished, and the stained glass windows were, Conrad Josefsen told her, apart from the Provincial Chambers in Christchurch, the only examples of medieval grisaille in all Australasia. On the wall behind the pulpit a brass tablet read:

'This church is erected to the
Glory of God
And in loving remembrance of
Andrew and Catherine Burnett
Who took up the Mount Cook Station
May 1864
And in the Wilderness founded a home.'

'This was raised by their daughters in this century,' Conrad told her.

'Why down here? We're only twenty miles from Timaru and you said a hundred and thirty to Mount Cook.'

'Good question. In ... let me see ... 1873, Andrew Burnett bought two thousand acres of land here at Cave and built a residence as well as retaining his property against the mountains. The Mount Cook property is still farmed by his granddaughter, who married St Barbe

Baker, the famous Man of the Trees. Andrew Burnett retired here and lived till his ninetieth year, in 1927. My
father remembers him. He took an interest in his land
and stock up to within a few days of his death. His
daughters lived on here just across the road. They called
their home here after Mount Cook, but by the Maori
name, Aorangi, the Cloud-piercer. Christabel, in the
early days that Andrew and Catherine Burnett knew, the
terrain was really a wilderness. Their little son was three
when the first woman to visit the station arrived, Mrs
Leonard Harper. He didn't object to the gentlemen of the
party, Mrs Harper wrote to her sister: "but he set up a
howl on seeing me—never before having seen any woman
but his mother, and no doubt believing she was the only
one of the species".'

No doubt Christabel's reaction to this was gratifying
to Conrad. She stood still and closed her eyes, trying to
visualise it.

They came to stand at the pulpit. Its foundation was
the hearthstone of the first habitation of Andrew and Catherine, in a V-shaped hut they occupied before their homestead was built. The top was exquisitely fluted and
carved from part of the prehistoric *totara* forest once
stranded in the Tasman Valley. It had a Bible-rest of
inlaid *kowhai* depicting mountain ribbonwood blossom
and mountain lily, and had a polish of unbelievable bril-
liancy. Christabel touched it with a fingertip in a tribute
to the excellency of the craftsmanship and the hours and
hours of loving toil.

They crossed to the baptismal font, marvelled at the
huge unhewn greywacke boulder from the Jollie River
Gorge, that weighed nearly four hundredweight and
which, in those distant days, had been carried by Andrew
something over a hundred yards when he was building
his musterers a hut in the Gorge.

Above it was a hub of the gigantic bullock dray the
pioneers had used on their first travels into the Tasman
Valley. But the focal point was the sandstone mortar that
held the baptismal water, a prehistoric mortar once used

for grinding oats or barley, something ages older than a quern. It had been brought out from the head of Strath Bora in Sutherlandshire to the coastline of the same county, by the Mackays, the Highland ancestors of the Burnetts. Perhaps a relic of dear familiar things carried away by them in the cruel days of the evictions.

Christabel looked from that prehistoric stone to the prehistoric *totara* and then to the inscription below the windows to the women of the Mackenzie country . . . 'who, through Arctic winters, and in the wilderness, maintained their homes and kept the faith . . .'

She said brokenly, 'Kept the faith . . . and saw things through . . . and built to last. But Lisa . . . how long was she married? Not two years. You'd have thought this country and these memorials might have kept her from— that.' Her voice trailed off. She looked up, blinking tears away, to surprise a strange look on that rugged face above hers. Conrad seemed jerked into speech, 'Then— you wouldn't—now——' he stopped dead. She said, 'I wouldn't now *what*?'

He shook his head and there was finality in it. 'Never mind. Some things are better not said. Let's go. It would be a pity to drive up the lakeside at Pukaki too late to see sunset on Mount Cook.'

For the sake of that truce Christabel asked no more.

By the time they reached Fairlie they could see the big fellows peeping over the top of the foothills and predominantly Scots names were appearing on the gates of the homesteads and lesser farms. The mixture of native and English trees delighted Christabel as she recognised oaks, larches, limes, elms among the evergreens she hoped to come to know. Rowans were reddening a little, sign of the approaching autumn, and now the real Mackenzie Country came into being as they threaded through Burke's Pass . . . chains of mountains, jagged-peaked, were tucked back in. They turned a bend in the road, a long straight stretch lay before them, a signpost said fourteen kilometres to Lake Tekapo and there, suddenly and dramatically, was their first view of Mount Cook.

It took her breath away. Despite his antagonism, his pride in the heights of this mountain country where he had been born and bred forced Conrad to display it to its best advantage. He drew to a stop, leaned across her and opened the door. 'You need to see it unimpaired by a honey-smeared windscreen. I'm afraid the bees have found it lethal today, and it's better, anyway, to breathe the air as well as look.'

True, the air was like wine. No fumes, no tobacco smoke, no chimneys, and the only sounds the occasional bleat of a sheep or the trill of larks in the sky. It had all the purity of the eternal snows and ice-falls in it, and the cleansing rivers, with a breath of tussock and wayside clovers. Beyond, rising in sculpted snow-ridges and slashing peaks, above other mountains that were in themselves great heights, rose Aorangi, glitteringly clad, but today there were no clouds to pierce, just silver-pencilled outlines against a blue canopy of sky. The brilliance hurt the eyes.

As they got back in the car he said, 'You were fortunate in your first glimpse. Sometimes the clouds veil it for days at a time. It will be a marvellous view today right up the lake. Pukaki is long and the road runs up the left side of it almost clean to the village. Once this road was rough and full of potholes and dust and coaches creaked and groaned along it. Now, with the advent of a huge chain of hydro-electric works, the tarseal goes right to the Hermitage. Lisa would have told you about that, of course. To her that great tourist hotel provided the one example of the life she craved. If only she'd come out to see how we lived before she married Rogan!'

'That's what Father and Mother wanted her to do,' said Christabel. 'Rogan didn't paint it other than it is, so he mustn't be blamed, but to Lisa, wanting to escape, a sheep station of fifty thousand acres spelt wealth, seven or eight thousand sheep a fortune in wool-clips and meat, plus the cattle.'

'To escape from what?'

She hesitated. His perception was keen. 'No doubt,

because she's so recently dead, this makes you feel dis-
loyal, but I'd like you to put me in the picture. I could
even try to understand.'

'I'll have to be frank. I think you know she came to
live with us after Jamie died. We did realise she needed
some life other than the domestic one. But she didn't pull
her weight. She was always exhausted, yet needing to go
out. It worked all right, till Mother's health began to fail.
Lisa knew the writing was on the wall, that the time had
come when she must take full responsibility for the children. Dad and I could manage to look after Mother.
Then Dad developed a bad heart. It was about then that
Rogan appeared on her horizon. He really fell for her.
When—when things were going her way Lisa could be
very charming. She could see months ahead of her in
shared nursing. She saw in Rogan a way out. Dad offered
to pay her fare out to see if she could take the life, but she
swotted up umpteen travel brochures, and the sound of
the glamorous life of a tourist area blotted out the true
everyday existence for her. And it's brought her to her
death. Worse than that, it's left Rogan broken in health
and spirit.

'As for the children—that reminds me. You said you
didn't want them more upset emotionally. I'll do all I
can to restore balance to heal the damage done, but I
think you'll have to allow a certain amount of natural
emotion when they see me. I mean, they may break
down. I was part of their world for so long. I feel it would
be more damaging for them to bottle things up. So please
don't go all hostile if they rush at me, and—and weep.'

He said heavily but not resentfully, 'I wouldn't have
done that. You're of one mind with Jonsy. She worried
about Davina. Hughie got it out of his system. Davina
went all tight-lipped and stoical. A sort of: "Well, let's get
on with living and put that behind us," attitude. No, if
she lets it rip when she sees you I won't be censorious.
What I dreaded was you unsettling the children, feeling
they must be swept back to London.'

They came over the hill to find Lake Tekapo below

them and near. It was like a Canadian village, nestling among pines with serrated edges and a host of trees unfamiliar to Christabel. The lake was a milky turquoise, so much so that she expected to see pinpoints of fire sparkling back from the surface as in an opal. At the edge half-submerged willows and pines still survived from when the level of the lake was raised, but the re-planting had been done beautifully, and wild flowers bloomed amidst the glacial stones of the hillsides, patching the red tussock with living colour, red clover, yarrow, daisies, scarlet pimpernels and some tall, rough-leaved plants with yellow blooms that reminded her of the mulleins in England's green lanes. Tall foxgloves wore fairy bells for flowers, and lupins in every hue of the rainbow, almost, ran rampant.

'Man enhanced nature here,' said Conrad. 'The upper Waitaki basin was indeed bare and inhospitable, with hardly a tree to break the monotony of the tussock. Trees had been here countless aeons ago, because there were small traces of coal, but by the time the Europeans arrived it was a stark, harsh land till the settlers began to plant trees, partly for fuel, partly because they needed shelter, but also because they were a beauty-loving people. They'd brought with them, through all the months of weary sailing, small, sturdy saplings, that finally resisted the elements and made a haven for birds, stopping the erosion of ice and snow and tearing winds, blizzards and droughts.'

Christabel spoke impulsively. 'Put that in a book some time.'

They went into a tea-rooms, beautifully appointed, at the rear of the store, and had tea and sandwiches. Conrad said, in a low voice, 'I won't introduce you. The discovery of the car in the river received wide publicity and you could be the object of natural curiosity. We're well known here.'

As she got back into the car Christabel paused, loth to leave the scene. What a holiday playground ... chalets dotted among the trees, a grand sweep of classical moun-

tains on the far side, a scarlet jet-boat with a girl in a
bikini curving behind it on water-skis in a sheer poetry of
motion. None of the scene seemed to have anything to do
with the tragedy that had brought her here.

They headed south, turning to the left, saw mountains
bare of snow, making a lilac rim to the horizon, and
headed through Simon's Pass. Beyond those lilac mountains they kept getting glimpses of high snowy alps back
in, westward, and every now and then the sharp triple
peaks of Aorangi itself. They seemed to be turning away
from it but would curve round to the foot of Lake Pukaki
where the glacier-fed waters would be harnessed to start
off the great chain of hydro storage lakes towards the distant Pacific. These lakes would feed both the North and
South islands with power.

Sad to think the historic coaching village of Pukaki was
no more, but when they came to the Lookout and
paused, as so many tourists were doing, it was hard to
imagine anything more beautiful on the glass-clear day,
those peaks against a sky almost cobalt, the iridescent
lake below, giving off blue and green facets, and, at the
left side of Aorangi, the magnificent glittering ice-face of
Mount Sefton, where the road would end.

Now, as they took the road uplake, the mountains at
the head were perfectly duplicated in the waters. 'It very
rarely happens,' Conrad commented, 'because the lake is
glacier-fed and the melt-water has rock-dust in it, but on
a day as still as this it settles and out come the reflections.
Not far to go now,' he added. 'We pass Mount Hebron
Station first, where the Macandrews live. Mary Macandrew, wife to Ninian, has been taking the children from
Thunder Ridge—shepherds' children too, I mean—for
their correspondence lessons since things began happening to us. But it will be even better with Barbara home.'

'Was that the Barbara your mother mentioned?' asked
Christabel. 'Who must have joined my plane at Fiji? She
was going in to see Rogan.'

'The same.' There was a tone of immense satisfaction
in his voice. 'Barbara is very special. She's the grand-

daughter of the old couple at Mount Hebron, and a true daughter of the misty gorges. That's the highest praise anyone can bestow here. She's been teaching in Fiji the last year or two. Like all of us, she got a bit unsettled. But now she'll be home to stay.'

A true daughter of the misty gorges ... not an alien like Lisa ... not a gatecrasher like Christabel ... Lucky Barbara who was special. She *belonged*.

CHAPTER FIVE

CHRISTABEL seemed mesmerised by that glittering ice-face of Mount Sefton, which grew remorselessly nearer. So soon now she would have to brace herself for what ever shocks and adjustments this new environment would bring her. All these elements seemed larger than life, intimidating in their immensity. Would the problems she faced be just as formidable in size, dwarfing her stature till she was unable to cope? Panic seized her. Then just as she felt she must turn to this hostile man beside her and beg him to understand, to stop classing her with Lisa, something she had read somewhere, some time, rose up in her memory. Something about finding stillness in the heart of the storm.

Her mind clutched at it, found comfort. Stillness was what she needed, not the flutterings of panic. She tried to recall what else it had said ... how deep within us, if we can but call on it, is the strength and calmness to cope with whatever is demanded of us at a given moment. Her pulses steadied. What did it matter if this man took out his hurt on her? He'd said Jonsy was understanding with the children, and he also seemed to be kindly disposed towards them. She could take anything as long as the children didn't suffer.

They turned a bend, and where the road curved back before twisting out to the lake edge again she saw immense gateposts, fashioned out of the stones of the hillsides, with what she called cattle-grids between them and what New Zealanders called cattle-stops.

The paddocks each side were tawny with tussock and Hereford steers grazed there, but on the heights above moved countless merino sheep, neat-looking, with snowy fleeces.

On each side of the posts were poplars in full leaf, but from there the great sweep of the terrain, reaching back into an infinity of mountain tussock land, was devoid of trees to soften the outlines.

As if he'd read her thoughts, as she lifted her chin to rake the entire panorama, Conrad said, 'The house is more than a mile back from here and when we get into the valley, the plantations begin. Larch, pine, Douglas firs . . . in the early days, when the first Josefsen came here, the winds were pitiless . . . no shelter . . . so nothing was more precious than their bundles of saplings, brought here, with their bedding, their tents, their few implements, on the first dray. That was all they had . . . tents in all this wilderness . . . and they had an early snowfall. But they made it . . . they created all this!'

They had turned round the shoulder of the hill and rose a little above the stream that came out between these twin hills in a narrow little gully. 'Those hills are named The Portals. They curved round to give a minimum of shelter from the off-lake winds.' There before them, in glorious sunshine, lay the valley, an enormous estate, it seemed to Christabel. The homestead was sheltered now from the force of the sou'westers by great trees, and they curved round in a huge arc, so that only the sunny north lay exposed. Great metal awnings shielded the windows from the fierceness of today's sun, but she noticed that the house was also built to catch every bit of that sun in winter, when, jammed up against these mountains that divided east from west, the sun would go down, as the children had informed her in their letters, very early in the afternoons.

Registering these things kept her mind off the painful meetings ahead. There was still some distance to go. She recognised the brand-new ranch-style farmhouse Rogan had built for Lisa, on its separate plateau, a newly-formed garden, not quite as bright as the other, about it, and beyond both houses was quite a cluster of farm buildings, stables, an old unused cow-byre, a long row of what she guessed from others on the way up, were the shearers' quarters, and further on, beyond an enormous woolshed and sheep-yards and dog kennels, a couple of cottages.

'Here's where we begin to play our parts,' said Conrad. 'The children have had their share of tragedy. Now they'll hope that with your coming, their little world will return to some semblance of normality. No need really to signal our arrival with a tattoo on the horn, with all that barking from the dogs, but I will just the same.'

Through the front door of the homestead they saw two figures emerge, running zigzag down the terraces, towards the row of car-sheds. As they swung up the final rise, Christabel said, chokingly, 'Even at this distance, Hughie is like his father, and Davina like my mother.'

'I realised neither of them resembled Lisa in the least,' and though his tone was expressionless, Christabel knew he was glad about that. So was she. There was evidently a strong bond between him and his older brother, natural when, as children, their playmates would be few and far between.

He drew to a stop. The children reached the lower steps and suddenly stopped. Christabel recognised this halt as sudden embarrassment sweeping over them. Nothing in their short lives could have prepared them for knowing how to handle a situation like this. In actual fact, she didn't know herself. But one must plunge. She stepped out, held out her hands, said, 'Here I am. What an absolutely gorgeous place to live!' And as they rushed towards her then, she caught them to her and hugged them as if this were a perfectly ordinary happening . . . an aunt from overseas arriving for a holiday.

Conrad busied himself with the cases and a carton or two of provisions his mother had put in the trunk, and said casually, 'I'll need a hand with these. And Granny put in some caramel bars, which you're not to have till after dinner. Hughie, you can manage this, can't you? Davina, this looks about your size load . . . up we go! And you can show your aunt which room is to be hers, once she's met Jonsy.'

No one would have guessed Christabel's heart was

hammering at her ribs as she followed them across the verandah and into a hall and along to the kitchen, a huge comfortable-looking room that had windows on three sides, one facing the front and the mountains beyond. Though those same mountains were nothing but a blur to Christabel.

Jonsy was turning from the stove, with a huge brown casserole, and Christabel immediately guessed she had planned that, so she didn't have to offer a hand in greeting. She didn't blame her. She would be cautious, with a sister of Lisa's.

Jonsy was well built, sandy-haired, with vivid blue eyes ... the sort of eyes that always looked piercing and shrewd. Her greeting was pleasant enough, but Christabel's ear caught the tremor that almost undermined its carefully casual tone and knew an instant sympathy for the woman. 'Well, I'm glad you got in before dark. Come away in for a moment before the children show you the room they got ready for you. You'll be tired, coming all this way.'

Conrad, following, said, 'Well, I'm too late with an introduction ... good. I got held up rescuing a lizard from that darned cat. From Peterkin.'

The children had come downstairs and their attention was diverted immediately. 'Where is it? Is it badly hurt?—the lizard?'

Conrad shook his head and dumped the cases. 'No, apart from having lost its tail, of course ... but tails in lizard circles are expendable. It'll grow again. It scuttled under the house through that broken ventilator grille. But listen to the cat ... howls of protest!'

They all laughed as resentful yowling rent the air. Jonsy crossed to the refrigerator, took out some milk, got a saucer, said, 'Give him this, quick, and a bit of liver. I had it ready cut up for their tea, but there wasn't a cat to be seen five minutes ago. That'll take his mind off.'

The children disappeared and Jonsy said, in a more natural tone, 'They're so easily diverted, bless them, at this age, which is right and proper. I've kept them busy all day.'

All the tenseness went out of Christabel and she said quickly, 'Oh, Mrs Johnson, I'm so thankful you've been with them. It was terrible being so far away. But I can see they've been all right. I'll try to cope as well as you've done.'

Mrs Johnson looked her straight in the eye, measuringly. 'It's all right, lass. The way those bairns have talked about you I kenned fine they'd be all right once you got here. I don't mean just recently, but all along. I've no doubt you've been a-feared of how I'd take it, another woman coming in, but I'm that glad of someone of their very own being here, you needna worry.'

Christabel's rush of gladness nearly broke down her control. 'You don't know what this means to me. I did dread just that. I feel such a gatecrasher, but there was nothing else I could do. Though I thought I'd just have to cope with the situation of a runaway mother and wife, not this tragic end. It's been a shock, but knowing *you* think I ought to be here will make all the difference.' Her hazel-green eyes encountered the penetrating blue gaze of the man she had known as Tod Hurst. His gave nothing away. Hers did, plus the way she had underlined her words to Mrs Johnson. Knowing *someone* felt she ought to be here.

He said, 'The children are pacifying the cat. I'll show you to your room. Which one, Jonsy?'

'The one between theirs, of course. They put a lot of time into helping me get it ready today.'

He picked up her two cases and she followed with her travel bag. The old homestead had such a Victorian air that at any other time Christabel would have been charmed. Pots of geraniums stood on small windowsills at the end of a side-passage and on an old treadle sewing-machine covered with a white cloth done in hairpin work was a flourishing maidenhair fern. Photographic portraits of past generations in dark oak oval frames adorned the walls on each side of the narrow stairway.

They turned to the right and the window at the end of that passage looked deeply into the cleft of the valley that led into the everlasting mountains, the ranges that seemed to have no end. Conrad opened the middle door and the sunlight, striking through two dormer windows, laid shafts of pure gold across an old-fashioned Persian-patterned carpet square surrounded by well-polished boards. There were twin beds in iron and brass, covered with snow-white honeycomb quilts with knotted edges that here and there bore signs of age in missing tufts. The children, overdoing things, had the room a mass of dahlias, tiger-lilies, Michaelmas daisies and ferns.

Conrad Josefsen put the cases down and stood looking at her. Again she was swept by unreality. Could this really be the man who had laughed and joked with her on that idyllic trip round the south-west counties? Who had rejoiced with her over every reminder of ancient history, who had quoted Tennyson to her? She had thought then what an expressive face he had, mirroring his every reaction to the impact of scenery and antiquity . . . she had been grossly mistaken, because all the time he had known who she was. Yet he had said that magic evening on St Catherine's Hill, above the dreaming town of Winchester, that he had something to tell her. Then he had changed overnight. Why?

She wondered vaguely if he had had mail from New Zealand when they got back to the hotel, that might have told him more of the way Lisa was behaving, and he had decided that enough was enough, that he wanted no more to do with anyone related to his sister-in-law who was breaking his brother's heart. A harsh judgment, but perhaps understandable. Anyway, there was nothing Christabel could do about that.

He said abruptly, 'Well . . . I suppose you find this too quaint for words? Smacks of the pioneering days, doesn't it? However, the new house has everything of the most modern, so when you inspect it, if you want to move there with the children, we won't put anything in your way.'

She felt stung to reply, to let him know she knew what he was getting at. 'The only reason I'd prefer the new to this, *Thaddeus*, would be if you made it too uncomfortable to stay under the same roof. My sole concern is for the children. They may love their rooms over there and want to go back. As far as I'm concerned, this would be ideal, especially as it has a door in each wall so I can get to either child easily, if they have nightmares, or need me. And it's even got a writing-desk.'

Her eyes went to a small table in the window with two drawers, a good broad top, set out with a blotter and furnished with writing-pad, envelopes, a ballpoint pen.

He looked at the portable typewriter she had set down at her feet. 'You won't expect to carry on doing typing for over there, surely?'

Her tone was dry. 'I shan't be neglecting the children for it, I assure you, but there were some unfinished odds and ends I was duty bound to tie up.'

Conrad shrugged. 'It wasn't meant for offence, but if you take it that way, I can't help it. It—it just seems incongruous here, that's all, typing London documents.'

'I'd have thought you'd have been the last to think that. You type manuscripts and send them off to your publisher. You'll still do it, I suppose, when you can spare time from the demands of the station?'

His mouth set ruefully. 'True. It weighs on me, somewhat, but right now, Rogan needs me here full-time.'

It was ridiculous to feel such guilt, but Christabel did. Her sister, it was, who had brought the station to this pass and disrupted more lives than Rogan's and her own.

Conrad said, 'I'll leave you to this. The bathroom's on the opposite side, middle door. You may need to freshen up or change, but Jonsy said dinner would be on very shortly.'

She would have preferred to change, but didn't want him to class her with Lisa, who didn't care whose timetable was upset as long as she could appear exquisitely groomed. Christabel brushed her hair back, grateful it curled up naturally at the ends, applied lipstick, touched her wrists lightly with lavender perfume for refreshing, went downstairs and got the children organised.

'After the dishes are done,' she informed them, 'you must show me round, just so I'm not a duffer if I have to take telephone messages to someone and don't know the woolshed from the hay barn.'

Hughie grinned. 'Nobody could be as dumb as that, Aunt Christie, there's always bits of wool and daggings in the woolshed and hay in the hayshed.'

Unexpectedly Conrad came to her assistance. 'Your aunt means that if anyone asks her to get some dog-tucker out of the dog-food freezer she'd better know where it is and where you put it to unfreeze, or dog biscuits . . . or wheat for the fowl, and where they lay their eggs. And what we call various paddocks.'

'She'd better learn to ride the trail-bike,' said Hughie, 'if she's going to tear all round the place looking for people.' The children then vied with each other remembering things their aunt should know. Hughie said, 'And you don't ever give the dogs raw offal. No, sir! If there's any liver there, that's for the cats. You'll get us into trouble with the hydatids inspector if you do, but perhaps he'd let you off knowing you were pretty green about things.

'We'll show you where the ditch is where we bury the rubbish. We don't call it a dump, because we prefer a long ditch. You don't have rubbish collections way out here, you know. Good thing. We never have strikes that way. We keep all the food scraps for the dogs or the fowls or the cats, and bury the other stuff. Dad uses a ditch-digger for scooping out the ditch and then filling it in.'

'And gates,' said Davina. 'It's a crime, a serious one, to leave gates open in the country.'

'That much I do know,' said Christabel meekly, 'but I'm beginning to feel there are so many pitfalls ahead of me I'll need to be accompanied every time I set foot out of the door.'

Jonsy laughed, 'It's mostly a matter of gumption, and I'm sure your aunt has plenty of that!'

Christabel saw Conrad's eyebrows go up. She had a feeling he didn't like Jonsy to approve of her. She'd show him! Jonsy took a tablecloth out of a drawer and started to leave the kitchen. Christabel's response was instant. 'Mrs Johnson, aren't we going to have our meal here in the kitchen? In this sunny window?'

Mrs Johnson looked a little sheepish. 'Well, I thought, for your first night, we should use the dining-room.'

'I'm here to do a job, not make more work. Let's just have it as you usually do. Children, you'll know where everything is, get the cutlery and other things and help me set the table while Mrs Johnson dishes up.'

A little of the tension began to go out of Christabel. The children began to chatter, Hughie the most naturally. Davina had great rings of shadow under the brown eyes beneath her fringe of streaky gold hair, making her look oddly unchildlike. It made Christabel's heart ache. She was glad their table manners were so good, something mainly due to her mother who had done so much towards their training. And she had to admit that though this man hadn't been with them much till now, they were completely at ease with him.

Hughie said, 'Uncle Conrad, did my dad like the drawing I did for him of Fleetfoot?'

My dad! Possessive and loving. How *could* Lisa have spoilt all this for her children?

'He sure did. When your granny came back from the hospital she said the nurses had stuck it on his bed-tray with some Sellotape. It's a movable sort of trolley-tray that goes right over the bed, and it's got an absolute wizard of a gadget on it for your dad, seeing he can't use his fingers yet, that turns the pages of his books for him.'

The little earnest face lit up. Christabel said, 'Is Fleetfoot Rogan's horse?'

Hughie shook his head. 'No, my fawn. Well, he's bigger'n a fawn now. His mother got shot and one of the deerstalkers brought him in. Dad's made a big enclosure for him.'

Unreality sat heavily on Christabel the whole time the beautifully cooked and served meat was eaten, the dishes washed, and the half-hour the children gave her outside, pointing out the various outbuildings to her and farm features. Christabel dissuaded them from taking her to the farm cottages; she didn't feel like meeting any other strangers tonight, either hostile or kindly, casual or curious. It seemed incredible that this could be February ... that the faint breeze coming through the valley could be warm, that it was late in the evening yet the light still lingered.

'Of course we've got daylight saving still,' said Davina, 'but at the end of the month the clocks go back an hour and we'll have lighter mornings and night will come sooner.'

There was a gravity about Davina that Christabel couldn't like. But she had to accept it. Time might break it up. No child of barely eleven should look like this. There was a watchfulness about her eyes that spoke of being wary of what life could do to you, tiny lines of control etched above that beautifully curved mouth, lines that were reminiscent of those about Christabel's mother's mouth, engraved there by the sorrows of her first marriage.

They turned their steps back towards the homestead, came up one or two terraces and at the corner turned to look due west. 'Oh, lovely!' cried Hughie, 'Look, Aunt Christie, God's turned the floodlights on Aorangi!'

It couldn't have been a more apt description, the flaming sunset they had turned their backs on just minutes before had fled the sky, leaving it steely grey and completely clear of cloud, but the sun, focusing on its snowy, triple-peaked grandeur, had lit up the whole gleaming whiteness of it with living flame. Christabel had never before seen such an intensity of light. It seemed to glow from within, rather than be just a reflection. She stood perfectly still in tribute, hands clasped in front of her.

Then she said slowly, 'That's a perfect way to describe it, Hughie. That's sheer magic. As if someone had decided to turn the full spotlight on the stage on to the biggest character of all. Not a single other peak is catching any of the light—they're all in shadow. You ought to put your description of that into an essay some time.'

Hughie laughed. 'Uncle Conrad said it first,' he confessed, 'but it fits, doesn't it?' As Christabel turned to her nephew she found Conrad himself there. He had come down the steps unheard. Their eyes met. How could a man be so kindred in thought, so hostile in action, so prejudiced? But you couldn't be petty in the face of all that wonder. 'Then, Hughie, I hope *he'll* put it in a book some time, so that other people, all over the world, will feel they've seen Mount Cook at its loveliest.'

Conrad said, 'That's what I'm trying to do, mentally, if not at my desk. So it's not all loss being away from my Auckland study. Aorangi has a thousand moods, but this has always, to me, been the fairest of all.'

All through the next hour it seemed incredible to Christabel that twenty-four hours ago, though she had been in turmoil of mind, she had thought of Lisa only as a runaway wife and mother, but the hours of today had brought her the bitter knowledge that for Lisa there were to be no tomorrows for repentance, and none either, for still more wilful destruction of all that Rogan had offered her, destruction of the harmony of this family, a sort of vandalism of the spirit.

Lisa was gone, the funeral was over, attended by none of her own . . . but Christabel put the children to bed, tidied away their things, tried to create for them a normal world out of bewilderment.

She said to Davina, lying back on her pillows, smooth long hair beautifully brushed, teeth cleaned, looking very precise and calm, 'I'll just go and read to Hughie for a while. He said he still liked being read to, then I'll come back to you and we can chat.'

She saw Davina's face harden against the suggestion, but she said politely, 'Oh, don't bother, Aunt Christie. Just spend the time with Hughie—he's so little. I'll read for about twenty minutes, then I'll put my own light off. I don't need to be tucked up any more.'

Christabel couldn't help making one bid to break down that too-adult composure. 'But your mother tucked you up, didn't she? So——'

There wasn't a tremor in the little voice. 'No, she wasn't often here. She had her own car and it's not far to Mount Cook Village. There's always something on there for the tourists. Dad always tucked us up. But I'm too old for that now.'

Christabel had to take it. 'Of course you are, Davina. Grown-ups never realise when children reach various stages. Goodnight, pet, see you in the morning.' She dropped a quick kiss on the petal-soft cheek, and walked out of the room, blindly.

When she had pulled herself together she went into Hughie's room. Bless him, he was always so uncomplicated. She sat on his bed, slipped an arm round him, let him read her a whole story, recognising that he wanted to show her how advanced he was now, in his reading. He got out of bed and showed her his collection of miniature cars, boasting a little in a sort of mini-masculine way because she was so dumb about makes and engines.

She read him a story till his short straight lashes drooped fanwise on his brown cheeks, then she turned him over, gently so not to waken him, and withdrew his hand from under his pillow so he would lie more comfortably. The hand came away with something in it, instantly recognisable, because Christabel had been familiar with it for over twenty years ... a little black golliwog, a knitted one, well darned because it had survived so many adventures ... the little golliwog that Lisa, then a loved and loving sister, had made the small Christabel. Hughie hadn't wanted his aunt to know he still liked to have Alphonse in bed with him.

Swiftly Christabel turned the light out, walked out of the room, down the stairs and straight out of the door on to the terraces above the valley floor into that alpine world of vast mountains and brooding silences. A pale moon and a myriad stars gave her enough light to see by. She walked on, grateful that there was somewhere to go till she could get control of herself again. She went down to where the creek sang along the valley floor on its way to the lake. She stopped on a small white-painted bridge, put both hands on the rails and let the tears have their way, sobbed it all out.

Suddenly she sensed she was no longer alone and was about to turn, stiffening, when he cleared his throat ... Conrad.

She did turn then and knew that in this clear light he would catch the silver glint of her tears. She said chokingly, 'I need to be alone, Conrad. I'll come in presently. Please respect my urgent need for privacy at this moment?'

He said, 'I will go, but not yet. Jonsy saw you as you came downstairs and sent me after you. She said you'd borne up almost too well and could be suffering from delayed shock—that though we were concerned more with the harm Lisa had caused, you'd lost a sister, and in the last year or so, both parents. Don't send me away right away. Jonsy would eat me. She'd think I'd bungled it.' When she didn't reply he added, 'Would words help? Is it because you had to keep up in front of the children?'

She caught a sob back and forgot his recent behaviour in her need for comfort. 'It wasn't the bearing up. I felt all hard and tight inside, and unforgiving. Most of all for what she's done to Davina. She's not all smashed up like Rogan, but she's got inward scars. She didn't want a chat, didn't want to be tucked up, said she was past that. I—I—simply hated Lisa in that moment for what she'd done to her child. And—my next thought was too horrible for words.' She shuddered as she remembered.

Conrad put out a hand, took her elbow, turned her right round to him, looked down on her and said, 'But I think you'll have to put it into words to dispel that bogey.'

Resentment flared within her. 'What are you? An amateur psychologist, or what? Or just plain curious?' She was lashing out, she knew, like a wounded animal.

'I did take psychology at university, yes. But right now I'm hoping it's plain old common sense. Something you learn in the university of hard knocks ... or just living here among the mountains. But if you really think it could be curiosity only, I'll go.'

Christabel bit her lip, put up both her hands to brush the tears away, and sniffed. Conrad put a large handkerchief into her hand. She used it, said, 'I'm sorry I said that. Perhaps it was a defence against admitting what I'd thought. I'd found myself thinking, when I saw what Lisa had done to Davina, that what had happened to her, and to that man, was poetic justice—a ghastly thought to harbour. Then I read to Hughie, and he fell asleep, and when I turned him over and pulled his hand from under his pillow to make him more comfy, it was clutching the tiny golliwog Lisa made me when I was five and she was fifteen. It just broke me up. It was only then that I realised that all that coppery beauty and fun and gaiety were gone, finished. When I was little she was such a loving sister. Only she had that selfish streak in her from my mother's first husband. And the older she got, the more it dominated her other qualities.' She buried her face in her hands.

Conrad's arms came about her then, not in a man–woman embrace but simply a comforting gesture of one human being to another. 'Let it go,' he said, as might the brother Christabel had never had have urged. She took him at his word, and wept it out.

Then it was all over. She lifted her head from his shoulder said, 'Thank you, Conrad Josefsen. I can cope now. I'm not usually such a watering-pot, nor as hard as to entertain thoughts like that. It's good for us, at times, to see ourselves as we can be. I don't want to be too hard on Lisa, or too sentimental about her either. All any of us can do here is to pick up the threads and try again.'

She used his handkerchief again, then gazed out over the scene and felt soothed by it. 'This,' she said, waving a hand at the glittering silver peaks, 'makes all our problems and anguish seem smaller. I feel now I can cope with tomorrow. I didn't when I first rushed out. Perhaps tomorrow is all I need to worry about, not the endless string of days ahead. If I thought it would make the situation here heal up more quickly, I'd take the children back to London with me, but tonight when Hughie asked: "How did *my* dad like my picture?" I knew it wasn't as simple as that. The children love him. They love Thunder Ridge and Mount Cook and Lake Pukaki and everything about the life here.'

They were both leaning on the rail now, looking down into the black waters of the creek, with only a gleam of silver where a ripple caught the moonlight as it washed over a boulder. Conrad said, 'There's also Rogan's side of it. He loves those children as his own. He's lying there worrying about how it's affecting them. You'll see, when he comes home. We'll play it along, as you say, a day at a time. I'm more hopeful of the outcome since——'

Christabel said, 'Go on. Since what——?'

He said slowly, 'Perhaps it's ridiculous to set such store on Barbara coming home. I'm probably clutching at a straw, but Barbara's going to act as governess to Mary and Ninian's children, to Davina and Hughie and to the shepherds' children here. Barbara is like her grandmother, Elspeth Macandrew, and she has the same gift Elspeth has ... my mother described it once as making you feel that God's in His heaven, all's right with the world. Barbara will help us all settle to some sort of normal living.'

Christabel remembered him saying Barbara was special. Special to everyone, it seemed. Was she also particularly special to Conrad?

Somehow they got through the evening, looked at television, something that was fairly recent up here where the mountains presented great technical problems. Jonsy said it had been a boon in the matter of keeping staff. 'The couples up here like to have it for their evenings together. I can understand it. I like it myself, though it seems a long cry from the early days, when even wireless was a miracle and a godsend. The pioneer women in these remote areas, especially the properties only reached by fording boundary rivers, sometimes didn't see another woman's face more than once a twelve-month and got stores about as often; when the wagons came in for the wool, they brought vast quantities of staple things ...

flour, sugar, rice, sago, tapioca, treacle, oatmeal. Most of the other things they produced themselves once they got their paddocks sown. Before that, they did without. Now we get pasteurised milk, papers, bread, mail, three times weekly.'

Conrad looked up from the paper he'd brought with him. 'And now the whole world comes to our door ... the mountain climbers from all over the world, the tourists, the guides, the ski-instructors ... any day in the village you can hear half a dozen languages.'

'Do the village houses go back to pioneering days?' Christabel asked.

'No, it's completely dominated by the tourist industry. It all belongs to that. In the old days there was merely the Hermitage, the first one built nearer Mount Cook, the second one destroyed by fire in 1957. The first had succumbed to flood forty-four years before. Only a few homesteads such as ours, and the ones on the far side of the lake, have their roots in the soil and rock.'

He went on making small talk, pushing the strangeness of his situation and hers, and the tragic circumstances, further away. It was the only thing to do, treat her as any visitor from overseas.

'Did you have any trouble getting your flight out here?' he asked. 'I'd have thought it might have taken you longer.'

'Oh, I've a friend who runs a travel agency—my best friend's husband. He'd do anything for me, Timothy Stennison. He was marvellous. I simply left everything to him. He even got me tenants for the flat—they were moving in about now. Tim suggested I stop over in Vancouver. I've an aunt there, Dad's sister, our only relation left. It was like waving a magic wand doing it through Tim.'

'You certainly were fortunate. Not many people would have had it so good.'

What made her suspicion a sarcastic dryness in his tone? As if she used people as Lisa had always done?

She said crisply, 'Not my personal charm, I'm afraid.

For his wife's best friend's sake, really. Just one of those things.'

'Just one of those things,' Conrad agreed, and Christabel saw Jonsy lift her eyes from a sock of Hughie's she was darning, and look at him in what Christabel felt to be a puzzled fashion.

He read the leading article aloud to them, then said, 'I expect they were sad to say goodbye to you. New Zealand isn't far in time now, but air-fares aren't cheap.'

She agreed, then added, 'But in this case, it's not quite so far out of reach. Timothy's well up in the travel business and takes familiarisation trips all over the world. I could see him out here some day. I know he's considering it.'

'You mean since you decided to come?'

'Yes. He's been once before, a long time ago, but he did say when I was leaving, not to feel too cut off, that I'd see him here one of these days. Just cheering me up, I suppose.'

'Would he bring his wife?' asked Conrad.

'I doubt it. The children are rather young, yet. Janice doesn't like leaving them with anyone, and if they came in their long holidays, it would be winter here.'

'Yes, and many men prefer to travel alone, anyway.'

Again something in his tone disturbed Christabel. 'Only because one's supposed to travel faster alone,' she pointed out, 'and he can't leave his business too long.'

Suddenly she felt awkward. Conrad probably thought she was planning a long stay. Perhaps living here altogether. That must be why he sounded so ... so what? So disapproving.

Nothing like length of stay could be decided at this stage, but it underlined for her, in spite of his kindness tonight on the bridge, that she was just here on sufferance, and that the future was certainly an unknown quantity for Christabel Windsor, for Davina and Hughie.

CHAPTER SIX

TOMORROW brought Christabel the knowledge that she was going to need all the courage and philosophy she possessed to pick up the threads Lisa had snapped, and to weave for the children some sort of normal family life. There were so many things to do that were painful.

One good thing was that Conrad disappeared with the children right after breakfast, to the Mount Hebron Station for their schooling. It was all of seven miles back on the road, but it seemed that these people, born and bred in the tradition of much greater distances over roads that had hardly been worthy of the name once, thought seven miles on tarseal, over creeks that were bridged now, meant nothing at all.

Christabel made her own bed and the children's, because Jonsy told her they made theirs only at weekends, as it was such an early start. She dusted and tidied those rooms, and fully unpacked her own things before Conrad got back.

Jonsy had made another pot of tea by that time and fresh cheese scones, dotted with chopped green shallot tops. 'I use spring onions when I've got them,' she said, 'but these do us all winter long for salads and sandwiches.' Christabel was surprised to find herself hungry. The mountain air must sharpen one's appetite, she supposed.

Jonsy poured herself another cup. 'You could postpone what you have in mind, Conrad, till later on. Perhaps even next week. There's plenty of work outside that's slipped back this last week.'

'No.' Her voice was crisp, inflexible. 'Better by far to get it out of the way. Painful but necessary, like surgery. Better not postponed.'

Jonsy looked unconvinced. He said, 'I think Christabel

is tough enough to take it.'

Jonsy said, 'Anybody would think you'd known her longer than just one day, to hear you.'

Christabel was annoyed to find her cheeks warm. She hoped no one noticed it.

Conrad began to speak, but Jonsy interrupted him. 'He wants you to go over to the new house and get those things out of the way that might upset his brother when he comes home. Better out of the children's way too, but I think it's hard on you so soon after arrival.'

Conrad said, 'How about it, Christabel? It can be your decision.'

That was nonsense, because in the face of a challenge like that, what else could she say but: 'Let's get on with it.'

Jonsy said, 'You'd better thank your lucky stars that this one has mettle, my lad. Not many would face it so soon. Off you go, then.'

As they neared the new house Conrad said, 'You must be the most disarming person I've ever met. I was quite prepared for Jonsy to be cagey with you to start with. But she's made up her mind pronto, which is unlike her, that you're a cat of a different colour.'

'Conrad Josefsen, I don't even begin to understand you!' exclaimed Christabel. 'What a contrary make-up you've got! I'd have thought it was evident that though Lisa and I shared a mother, we were as unlike as it's possible to be. I don't mean it to sound priggish, but it's a fact. Mrs Johnson didn't make a snap decision. She said very frankly that from what the children said about their aunt, I wasn't like Lisa. Look, being in Auckland, you wouldn't know as much as she did. She knows I'm different.'

He said heavily, 'I hope she never has any reason to change her mind.'

Christabel kept her tone even. 'I can't think of any answer to that. Of any reason why you might think she should. I sincerely hope you aren't bigoted enough to *look* for similarities! Let's just get on with this distasteful task which it seems we must do together. Tell me, why is it so urgent to you? From what you said about Rogan, it could be weeks before he gets back up here, even if he's allowed to convalesce with your parents in Timaru.'

'I'm not sure. As soon as he's any way fit, he'll move heaven and earth to get back here. The rooms must be rearranged.'

She felt a great unease for the children. How would they react, coming back here, without their mother?

'Conrad, the homestead is so large, won't they just stay on there? And won't Rogan need looking after by Jonsy?'

'I don't know what he'll want, but I've an idea he'll want the children with him wherever he decides to live. I'd imagine, anyway, that Mother and Dad will come up with him at first.'

'Then in what you're planning, where do I fit in?'

'We'll have to wait and see. Could be, if they came back here, that Mother and Dad would find them a bit much, and you could take them off their hands a bit.'

She felt the strongest impulse to say: 'I don't need a job created for me,' but checked it. He was high-handed, this Conrad Thaddeus Brockenhurst Josefsen. Perhaps Rogan would have other ideas. The children might need her for long after their father came home. But none of it was going to be easy. She was going to feel the interloper, the constant reminder of her half-sister.

They came on to the patio at the front, set out with cedarwood garden furniture, charmingly suggestive of long hot days and cool evenings. Christabel gained the top, turned, looked straight through the cleft, to another view of Aorangi. This time two of the peaks were hidden behind the other so that it seemed to soar even higher. To its left the sparkling ice-face of Sefton, terrifying in its solidity, spelt out what looked like a warning ... thou shalt not pass beyond me. How odd to feel that, when one knew climbers went far beyond, but it still threatened. From here, one could not dream that below those two giants nestled the gay village of the alpine postcards Lisa had sent, with all the luxury of first-class tourist accommodation, exotic meals, gatherings of people from every quarter of the globe. Even so, it hadn't been enough for Lisa.

Conrad said, 'Incidentally, when Barbara Macauley comes to Mount Hebron, the schooling of the two families, under her, may take place at this homestead. I talked it out late last night, on the phone with the Macandrews. Mary and Ninian's children are older than ours, mainly. Barbara drives and it would help tremendously while Rogan's laid off, if I didn't have to do that fourteen miles a day, or anyone else, and there are four other children here belonging to the shepherds. It's better for their mothers to have them here. We've an old schoolroom at the homestead—I don't think you've seen it yet. The kids use it as a playroom.'

Christabel studied him as he gazed at the mountain. He was the younger son, had lived away from home a long time, but he was arranging the lives of this family and the Macandrew family as if he had the right. She said, 'The Macandrews didn't ask for time to think that over? Some people——'

'Oh, we'd planned this earlier, if Barbara would come. Mary and Ninian know how much it means to me to have Barbara here. It's the one compensating thing about the whole wretched business.'

Christabel turned away. 'Now, let's get on with the job in hand. If we're to remove all traces of Lisa, then we must do it in the hours the children aren't here.'

It was a dream house . . . how could Lisa have thought of leaving it? Rooms opened into each other, cunningly-wrought corners and alcoves held indoor plants that were mainly alpine ones brought in from the mountainsides and forests, feathery ferns, silver-leaved creepers, some bright with berries, to compensate for the time when every leaf in that gay garden outside would be encased in snow; the hearths were of the multi-coloured stones of the glacial valleys, pictures painted by some of the country's best known high-country painters graced the walls, lamp brackets placed to light them to best advantage or to shed rosy lights upon those who read beneath them in the deep modern chairs. Some lamps, cunningly interspersed among the others, were kerosene-powered, Christabel noted, reminder that in times of blizzard, power might be cut.

It gave her a pang to notice that Rogan must have bought all new furniture of elegance and taste . . . everything to keep a wife like Lisa happy. But much of the surroundings spoke of Rogan rather than Lisa, especially in the many bookshelves and the multitude of books that filled them. The children's rooms were delightful—no wonder they had so identified themselves with this life. But when they came to the master bedroom Christabel was filled with a great anguish. Not for the loss of her sister, but for Rogan, who must come back to this . . . more of a boudoir than a shared bedroom . . . Lisa's more than Rogan's.

Christabel supposed it was beautiful . . . that ornate shell of a bedhead, the white and gold of it, to frame Lisa's red-gold hair and topaz eyes . . . the greeny-gold sheen of misty draperies in spread and valance, the frilled and shirred pillows banked against the long tasselled bolster, the immense bevelled glass that took up almost all one wall, the dressing-table on which stood an array of creams and perfumes that could have stocked a beauty parlour. The carpet was white shag—how eminently unsuitable for a man to come into after being called out to move stock to safety during a treacherous thaw or torrential rain! Oh, Lisa! But to an injured man, coming back to these ultra-feminine fripperies, alone and bereaved, what would it mean?

She clasped her hands together in acute distress. 'What *can* we do about this room, Conrad? We *can't* have him come back to it. Even if he's been disillusioned, there'll be memories. It could have been so different had it been an ordinary bereavement. Time heals that, to a certain extent. I mean, we can get rid of that ridiculous range of cosmetics, and of her clothes, but the bed, the draperies, that satin pouffe. . . .'

She saw the jaw tighten, the blue eyes glint, but with determination and—she thought—satisfaction. 'I believe you're with me. Even if it seems high-handed, I'm going to risk being told that and get rid of it. This house hasn't anything like the number of bedrooms ours has . . . which just grew and grew as need arose, so Rogan will need this room—if not now, then someday. I'd like to get rid of these things, carpet and all. I know a firm in Timaru who'd jump at the chance of having it to sell. I'll pay for having it re-carpeted myself—the November royalties were good. And I'll bring over Rogan's stuff from his old room back home. What do you say? Am I taking too much on myself?'

Christabel's heart lifted. He was actually asking her advice! 'I think we'll both risk being thought high-handed, but how about if we share the blame? I think there's a strong link between you and Rogan, isn't there? Strong enough to stand a minor dispute, but if he thought her sister felt it wise too, it could help. He'd know we did it to spare him pain. Besides, he must think it's pretty fine of you to step into the breach like this, when you have your own work, your own life, up in Auckland. I admire you myself for that.'

He shrugged. 'I'm not as noble as you think. I'm sure two lots of genes war in me—my forebears here on Thunder Ridge and my mother's father at his editorial desk. I'm a compulsive writer, sure, but I absolutely revel in being out among the tussocks and the sheep again.'

More of the tension went out of Christabel. 'There's just one thing. You ought to bring Mrs Johnson into this. You said Rogan was like a son to her. Ask her opinion.'

He nodded. 'I'll get her over now. It's the biggest thing to decide. I'll ring her from here.'

While he was busy Christabel picked up one of the cartons he had sent over earlier. She must plunge, be matter-of-fact. It was sad at any time to dispose of a loved one's personal belongings, sadder still when that member of the family had left them not only by death but before that had destroyed the trust and harmony of the family circle. In they all went, the perfumes, the sprays, the lotions. She picked up a piece of paper that had lined the boxes, spread it over them and hid them from her sight.

She opened a drawer. It was almost empty. Only the shabbier things had been left, if indeed these could be called shabby, because to come out here Lisa had bought herself a complete trousseau, paid for by Rogan. The next box was filled in no time. Christabel slid back one of the wardrobe doors—Rogan's. She crossed to the other. What was left underlined for her the fact that Lisa had finished in a most definite way, with life among the mountains. Here were the outdoor clothes, elegant jodhpurs, brogues, shirts . . . not really things in which a wife might help work down at the pens, the sheds, the garden, but obviously she would have no use even for these in the new life she had thought to enter. She began flinging them into another carton, then thought of something. She ought to go through the pockets in case there were any papers in them Rogan might need, even if it was more likely things of that nature would be in her handbags.

She pulled out from a jacket, a couple of handkerchiefs, a docket for things purchased in the village, a crumpled headscarf, a piece of paper. She spread it out, took in its contents in a brief and horrified glance. She felt sick. It read:

'Darling, All's well. The Pass is open again. Tomorrow you'll be away from all this, a setting that doesn't suit you at all. We'll do Australia first, really living it up. You need a few weeks' break before you send for the children. If you must—as I've said, they might want to stay on the farm. Then for Hong Kong—wonderful life! And I've got what it wants to live well there. Lots of travel in it for you, too—you'll enjoy that. My business takes me all over the world. Don't back out now, it would break me up. Burn this. I want nothing to frustrate us now.—B.'

Careless Lisa, who'd not bothered to burn it. The Pass would be the Lindis Pass. Conrad had said they hadn't thought of them doing that, because it had been closed by a slip. They had gone through to Lake Wanaka and by the Haast Pass intending, no doubt, to travel up the West Coast and through Arthur's Pass to Christchurch, for the Sydney plane. Yes, one landslip had been cleared, but another had been waiting for them, on the West Coast. And had taken them to their deaths in the river.

She was still standing there, bleakly, when Conrad came back into the room. She held it out to him, wordlessly.

He read it, lifted his head and looked at her. 'Well?'

'She went with him, even when he said *that*—that the children could be happier left here. I find that unforgivable. I can understand Lisa being swept off her feet by his promises, by the lure of a life like that. But to desert her children . . . *no!*' Her voice became crisp. 'That settles it. No more nostalgia for me. No looking back sentimentally, to our childhood. No grieving. We're picking up the pieces she smashed. I won't allow myself to be unhappy, to be maudlin. Let's get on with it.'

She was surprised when Conrad came across to her and took one of her hands. 'Christie, I don't think we can afford to shut our minds—our hearts if you like—to any good thoughts, any happy memories. It does seem unbelievable that knowing Burford Grosset didn't want the children, she'd have risked going with him. But give her the benefit of the doubt, she might have thought she'd win him round. So don't cut out the more worthy memories, otherwise the past will be spoiled as well as the present.'

Christabel felt bewildered. This was the man who had seemed so harsh, who hadn't wanted her here because he thought she was probably tarred with the same brush. The man who had seemed so kindred as they had toured the old ways of England together, who had kissed her in the Vale of Avalon and among the trees on St Catherine's Hill . . . who had seemed to promise them a future together, then had just disappeared. What a complex character, what a formidable mixture, stirring you to resentment one moment, disarming you the next by such understanding. She hated herself for the feelings she found it hard to control, the physical feelings that were stirred to life in her by his touch. She didn't want to feel desire for this man who blew hot, blew cold. But she was thankful for what he had just said.

She nodded. He said, 'No one else must see this. Not even Jonsy. She's not coming over, anyway—thought we'd be better on our own. But she agrees we should get rid of all these frills and furbelows—said when she came back home when her baby died at birth, she was grateful that her mother and husband had taken away the bassinet, the layette, the pictures on the walls above the cot. So she spoke from experience.'

It helped. There were other people to be thought about besides Lisa. 'And did Jonsy never have another?' asked Christabel.

'No. That's why Rogan meant so much to her. Mother never begrudged her that. She really shared Rogan. He nearly died during the time Mother was so ill, in his first year. But for Jonsy he mightn't have lived. But she's not a bit possessive. She made no mischief between him and Lisa—in case you wondered.'

They worked steadily then. At lunch-time Jonsy brought over a meal for the three of them. 'I've rung Timaru, Conrad, and they've got the carpet that covers the rest of the house, as you suggested, and they had the measurements for the whole house originally, so they'll send someone up with it in three days' time, to take up the shag carpet, and lay the other. I haven't dismantled any of the things in Rogan's old room back over yet. The children would notice. Time enough to do it when the new carpet's laid. They'll be at Mount Hebron the day it's changed over. By the way,' she added, 'you needn't break off to go for the children. Ninian and Mary are coming over to meet Christie. I told them what she's like, you see, and they want to make her feel welcome to the district. They're over the moon about Barbara coming back, of course. They had a feeling she might never return.'

'Was she getting too fond of life in Fiji, then?' asked Christabel, simply for something to say.

'Not particularly. She liked it well enough, though it could have been she sounded that way in her letters so they wouldn't think she was homesick. To make her folks think she was picking up the threads again. Things'll go back to normal. First Conrad went away, then Barbara—a real parting of the ways.' Jonsy seemed to think of something and looked directly at Conrad. 'Did she know you were back when she set about leaving there?'

'I doubt it. Perhaps she always had it in mind that she could governess here, and Rogan's accident would tip the balance. She'd think we'd be in a devil of a hole with transport and what-have-you.'

Jonsy and Conrad seemed to understand each other and the situation. There was something behind this. Jonsy washed up, stacked the crocks away, then departed, saying over her shoulder, 'They'll not be here till four. Don't let the bairns catch you here. They're settling in reasonably well at the old house, and no wonder. It's more homelike for youngsters. They like even the old portraits. Odd how most youngsters do.'

Conrad said to Christabel, 'Children like continuity. A succession of generations spells stability. Youngsters like tales about their parents' childhood, tales of their surroundings in days gone by. Take Hughie. He could be Rogan's own son, and my nephew. He's identified completely with the life here. I was staggered when I came down for a fortnight after being overseas. He knew as much as I did about the early days here. Says things like: "At one time, of course, before four-wheel drive vehicles, we had to transport fence-posts on horseback and where horses couldn't go, by man-power." It's right. Children can adopt a heritage. Like Rogan being Jonsy's son in spirit, if not in flesh and blood. They belong.'

Yes, Conrad definitely saw the children's future as here. But where was Christabel's future? What was there for *her* here? Jonsy could see to the children's material needs. Rogan needed them to fill up empty hours for him. This Barbara would see to the children's education. If she hadn't turned up right now, it was conceivable that they would have looked to Christabel to oversee the correspondence lessons of the two big sheep stations. Plenty of outback mothers had to do it, somehow coping with their household tasks too, but what was *she* going to do?

She'd have to keep herself somehow, but how could she earn money? Her keep wouldn't matter, she knew, but there was more than that involved. She couldn't be just a parasite. Nor could she expect to be kept if she shut herself away in her room and worked on novels. Besides, not even one novel was out yet, and she'd spent her nest-egg on the trip out, and she must hold the return fare, in case she had to go back. New Zealand's laws on immigration were strict now, she believed. Every case was judged on merit. She'd probably have to show she was needed, when her temporary stay was over. She felt a flutter of panic, a fear of the unknown. She wanted to be with her niece and nephew, but were the members of this family likely to want her here? A blackness settled on her spirits, but she knew she mustn't show it. Take a day at a time, she told herself, just as she had through those long days, weeks, months, nursing her parents. Then the future will take care of itself.

When the Macandrew family arrived and tumbled out of the big estate car with Davina and Hughie, things became ordinary, the tragedy receded into the background. The children were hungry and full of high spirits after hours at lessons, and when Jonsy had satisfied their appetites at a table set out on the verandah for them, laden with fresh pikelets spread with redcurrant jelly and cream, fudge balls that were a mixture of minced dried apricots and biscuit crumbs, coconut and condensed milk, they disappeared in the direction of the play-paddock where were goalposts, a cricket pitch, swings, slides, seesaws.

'Look at our Rosemary!' groaned Mary. 'To think that the first few hours after she was born, I lay in a happy daze planning a daughter in frills and sunbonnets . . . all she wants to do is make herself as proficient at boys' games as Iain and Angus! Did you hear what she called out as she rushed off? "Let's get out the Rugby ball!" And that on a hot February day!'

She had a faint accent, not American, but—'Canadian,' said Mary, 'Canadian of Highland descent. I was Mary Rose, and the Roses came from Inverness way.'

'And were you a tourist here?' asked Christabel. 'Was that how you met Ninian?'

'No, we met in Singapore. I was nursing there and had to deal with cheeky New Zealand soldiers for my sins. I escorted this wounded Kiwi soldier home.'

'Your surname was Rose and you called your daughter Rosemary—how lovely!'

'Not quite the combination of my first name and surname, though that pleased us too. Rosemary was called after Ninian's little sister who didn't live to grow up.'

Ninian, talking to Conrad, turned his head. 'And my father fell in love with my nurse . . . with her name, her looks . . . my little sister had the same Highland colouring, black hair, blue eyes . . . and the moment Mary arrived, she helped him deliver a little black filly that was having trouble entering the world, so he thought she was his little Ros Mhairi reincarnated. So I married the wench to please him!'

Conrad chuckled, 'Watch it, Nin! I was about thirteen when they married, Christabel, and I heard a great tale from that Mrs Anderson who was the wife of one of our shepherds then. She was telling Jonsy how romantic it had been . . . just like on the films, she said. Andersons' little girl was being chased along the road by a bull. Mary was coming along in her car, got between the child and the bull and charged it. Believe it or not, Mary knocked that bull clean out! But Ninian was coming along the road behind her, in another car, like a bat out of hell, Mrs Anderson said, and he must have died about a thousand deaths.

'Mrs Anderson enjoyed telling Jonsy all about it, didn't she, Jonsy? Said that what followed was terrific. By Jove, I've not thought of this for years, Ninian. I wish you'd give me permission to use it in a book. He shook her and kissed her and went on something fantastic, Mrs Anderson said. She reckoned that if they'd not been engaged before they left Singapore, she'd have sworn he was proposing!'

The looks on Ninian's and Mary's faces were ludicrous. They all stared. It wasn't just embarrassment, it was almost guilt . . . it was rueful . . . almost as if they'd been caught out. Conrad said, 'By heavens, there's something fishy here . . . have I struck the nail on the head? What *was* happening . . . come on!'

Ninian held up a hand. 'What transpired was entirely between Mary and myself. We've never satisfied vulgar curiosity about that incident.'

Conrad said shrewdly: 'Why were you in separate cars? Was Mary running away from you? But where would she run to? The road ends against the mountains.'

Jonsy said in a tone that reduced Conrad once more to the stature of a thirteen-year-old stuffing himself with goodies at a wedding reception and listening in to gossip: 'Conrad, that'll be enough of that! Authors shouldn't pry to that extent. And what Christie will think of us all I don't know. She'll think you have no manners whatever.'

He was helpless with laughter. 'I sure have enjoyed this! Ninian was always taking me in hand when I was a youngster, and I've put him out of countenance for once.'

Ninian grinned, said, 'I'll take pity on you . . . no, don't sit up all eagerness. All I'm going to tell you is that Mary and I got our wires crossed and—she got a stupid idea into her head about—well, my past allegiances. And *her* past . . . in the shape of a former fiancé, plus *my* former Colonel, was rushing towards her from the Hermitage. She was trying to stop them calling in at Mount Hebron. And the bull solved everything. Seeing her in hideous danger made me articulate. I could have thrown a garland of daisies round that bull's neck, bless him. And that's all you're going to know. Now, are we going to attack our pikelets and fudge balls, or aren't we? I'm starving!'

After that there was no restraint. Christabel couldn't feel these folk were strangers. Under cover of the tea-table chat, Mary said to her, 'I expect, like me once, you feel a little like the odd man out, among a family like this, whose roots since the 1860s have been here? But you won't for long. How wonderful it is for the children to have their long-loved aunt with them.'

Christabel's eyes widened. 'You knew of me? Before I came?'

Mary said, 'Particularly at first. They talked to my children a lot about you, and I felt I knew you. Do you mind if I say I never got to know Lisa closely, though for Rogan's sake I tried? For her own—at first. But she thought I was clean dippy to settle down in what she called a God-forsaken spot, after living in Singapore. But Singapore isn't all night-clubs and entertainment and duty-free shopping, you know. Like Hong Kong it has its thousands and thousands of the very poor. There are sights any day to wring one's heart. And it sounded to me as if you'd had the thick end of the stick, left to nurse your parents without any backing-up or sharing from Lisa. So we're glad you're here.'

There was quite a buzz of conversation between Ninian, Conrad and Jonsy. They could have been alone, Mary and Christabel. Mary saw the hazel eyes grow troubled. 'What is it? Tell me, Christie.'

Christabel said, 'I came out not knowing what to expect, knowing only that Lisa had run away with someone. I didn't know how Rogan would react, whether he'd want the children or not. It wasn't a situation I could think my way through, at that distance, so I upped and came. I even thought the children might be regarded as nuisances, that they might be made to suffer for their mother's peccadilloes. I thought I might take them back to London if Lisa didn't contact them soon—that when she did, she could be told I had them. But now I find they adore Rogan, and are very fond even of Conrad, in this short time. Jonsy is wonderful with them,' she went on. 'Though she's getting on, she mightn't always be able to do it. Please don't misunderstand me, but it would have been less complicated had it been otherwise. I'd just have taken them—a clear-cut issue. For the first time in their little lives they're completely secure, loving the life here, having a father.'

Mary had a frown between her brows. 'Wouldn't it be an easy decision? Simply stay here. Must you go back? Are there ties? Someone you care for?'

'No, there's no one. But I feel superfluous. They're talking about Barbara, your husband's niece, coming to be governess to the two estates. Oh, don't say anything about this to her when she arrives. She's a trained teacher, and can do far more for them than I can. But I'm wondering how I'll fit in here, what I can find to do.'

Mary didn't minimise the problem. 'I can understand exactly how you feel ... because you've just got here. You haven't had a chance to sum things up. Sometimes these big estates are so busy with seasonal work, another pair of hands—woman's hands—are a godsend. The shepherds' wives help at shearing, harvest, lambing, but in the main they're fairly busy with their own families and gardens, plus feeding animals and so on. They have babies they can't leave, at times. Jonsy is marvellous, but even when her husband's here—Nat's away just now—it's a big house to manage and now she'll be cooking for Rogan again.

'I'm guessing Conrad will stay on for a few months till his brother's a hundred per cent fit again. I think you'll find you're very necessary.' She stopped, thinking of something. 'You're wondering what you'll do for money, aren't you? This station could easily put you on their payroll and never notice it. Talk it over with Conrad. You'll find him very understanding. Tell him I suggested it. He'll sort it out. Will you?'

The blue eyes and the hazel eyes met, consideringly. Mary said, 'You don't want to, do you? Why?'

Christabel made up her mind. 'Mary, if that scene of a few minutes ago hadn't happened, I mean when Conrad dropped his clanger about you and Ninian and the bull, I wouldn't have been able to tell you this, but—well, it so happened Conrad and I got off on the wrong foot, too.' She paused. She couldn't, with him just a few paces away, tell Mary how they first met, how inexplicably and contemptibly Conrad Josefsen had behaved. It wouldn't be right among friends of long standing, anyway. But she would tell her part-truth.

'You see, when this happened, Conrad wrote to me, returning a letter I'd written to Lisa, unknowing. All he knew then was that she'd fled with this man and he told me about Rogan's accident. I was horrified, of course. I rang him that night and offered to come to the children. He absolutely forbade me to come. I've got to be honest about him . . . there's a lot I can admire in him, but at that moment he was very harsh, judgmental. He thought I'd be like Lisa. I—came just the same, in direct defiance. He didn't know I was coming. You can imagine how he felt when I rang from Christchurch. I'd no thought other than to take the children away from a place where they would no longer be wanted. Now do you see why I can't ask him to put me on the payroll of the estate?'

Mary Macandrew shot to her feet, said quickly, 'Christie and I are off for a while. We've other things to talk about besides hay and dipping and whatnot.' She had Christie outside before anyone could offer to accompany them.

Mary chuckled, 'This is as much for my sake as yours. I've got such active tear-ducts. I didn't want anyone to ask what was the matter with me.' Christabel gazed at her. Mary continued, 'It's because I understand so well what it's like to be suddenly pitchforked into an isolated area like this, vast and magnificent and—worried about your place in the scheme of things, and your future— away from all that's dear and familiar to you. I was in a very false position too. I can't be frank about it because it concerns someone else very closely, but though outwardly I appeared to have a future . . . as Ninian's fiancée I was expected to be his bride. But all the time I was anything but sure he cared for me, so my life was hideously complicated too. Isn't this odd? I've never told anyone this much, till now.'

Christabel said, 'Thank you for that vote of confidence. I need something like that very much just now. I won't breathe a word. But at least *you* aren't classing me with Lisa. Neither did Jonsy. I can't altogether blame Conrad for thinking we could be birds of a feather, but it stings.'

Mary said, satisfyingly, 'But that would be grossly unfair and it just doesn't sound like Conrad.'

Unthinkingly, Christabel said, 'I couldn't believe it either. He seemed to have changed so.' The next moment she'd have given anything to have caught the words back. She'd given away the fact that she had had some preknowledge of him. But fortunately Mary was too intent on disabusing her mind of any idea that Conrad was really like that. 'Christie, you're still in a state of shock, though you don't realise it. And so would Conrad be when you rang him. It turned his life upside down too, don't forget. Don't make any snap judgments, or read into any ill-phrased words on an international phone call, things that are really foreign to his true nature. I've known him since he was a high-school boy. I've liked what I've known, and have seen him develop into a worthwhile man.

'I *can* imagine that in the first flush of his resentment against Lisa, he might think he wanted no more complicated relationships here and he might have felt you might upset the children, dividing their loyalties. He'd know Rogan needed them. We were all thrilled to see what a bond grew between Rogan and his stepchildren. But now you're here, the thaw must set in. Don't worry about Conrad.'

Christabel looked towards the daunting face of Mount Sefton and said, 'I don't know ... isn't there ice packed there, into those rocks, that never melts, year in, year out?'

Mary said sturdily, 'True, but as you say, that's been there a long time. This is just a sudden prejudice, not capable of lasting. Born of this situation. Look, when I arrived at Mount Hebron first I couldn't see ahead. I felt it would be no time before I must leave this land, far below the Equator, and go back to Canada, make a new life for myself without Ninian. But each day the ties that bound me to the Macandrew family grew stronger. Take it a day at a time. Something will resolve itself. At the moment you're needed here. In school hours they were so different today, *even Davina*. Perhaps if you feel you must, later, you might get a job at the Hermitage or Glencoe Lodge. They're often looking for staff. What did you do in London?' she added.

'Mostly typing. I wouldn't mind anything as long as I could stay near. Though it could be if this was fairly public—I mean the discovery of Lisa and that guest in the river—that they wouldn't want to employ me.'

'It wouldn't amount to much,' said Mary. 'Some of them up there might have wondered. Lisa was often seen in Burford's company, but sometimes Rogan was with her. It was Burford's third visit, but there's so much come and go up there, he was just one among many. He had visited the homestead here. Some people must have thought he'd probably just offered her a lift through the passes for a chance of seeing Fox Glacier and Franz Josef Glacier on the other coast. It was classed as death by misadventure. He was a lone wolf, a wolf in every meaning of the word, so there was only a sister in England, and business associates and friends in Hong Kong. The police informed everyone. So all you'd get from the people in the tourist village would be sympathy, I'd guess.

'A woman has an accident on a night of terrible storm. Her only relative flies out from London, takes on the care of the children till the stepfather comes out of hospital and the homestead goes back to normal. What more natural than that the sister should seek a job in the nearest place, to keep an eye on them? Do you realise that some of the day workers come from as far away as Twizel, the hydro-village way down past the foot of Lake Pukaki? Give it time, Christie, for everyone to recover from the shock of it all.'

Now Christabel was having trouble with *her* tear-ducts. The whole landscape shimmered before her. She laughed, took out her handkerchief and said, 'That makes two of us. Thank you, Mary. Things don't seem so black now, and regarding what you told me about your engagement . . . I'll never break that confidence.'

'I knew that. I didn't need to ask you to promise. Oh, here they come . . . just look at Rosemary! She's torn her jeans from A to Z. She's in dire need of a safety-pin. I hope you can find one.'

For the first time Christabel felt free of that weight on her spirits. 'I think we can do better than that. She and Davina are two of a kind as regards size. I'll lend Rosemary a pair of hers.'

'Not new ones, the oldest you've got. I know my Ros Mhairi.'

Jonsy wouldn't let them go without an evening meal. 'When I knew you were coming, I popped an outsized casserole in and took some apple-pies out of the freezer to thaw. It's a long time since we had you all to tea.'

The unreality that had possessed Christabel ever since she had got Conrad's letter began to disappear. This was a new life, and it could be she might find a niche here if some job offered at the village. Though nothing could be done till Rogan was well and home again. Earning money didn't matter for a few weeks.

From the talk at the table, they certainly needed to get back into routine work again. Ninian had been over here helping while Conrad had been in Timaru seeing to matters over the funeral and the inquest, though they weren't specifically mentioned.

Conrad said, 'One thing, it's no hardship to be out at the crack of dawn this time of year and we can get the stuff in while the weather lasts.'

Christabel, feeling more natural, said, 'Would you trust me with one of the cars? I could deliver the children at Mount Hebron. That would save you some time.'

Davina looked across at Conrad. 'She's a good driver, Uncle Conrad. Even drives in inner London, something Granddad wouldn't do.'

Conrad nodded. 'Okay. You can take the Holden station wagon. I'll put you through its paces after we've had coffee. You can take a few turns round the farm roads. It'll be light for ages yet.' He added, as to any newcomer, 'The further south you go in New Zealand, the longer twilight there is. Round Lake Te Anau, for instance, in midsummer, with daylight saving, it's light till nearly ten-thirty. Like Scotland.'

Ninian said, 'What a pity you and Christie hadn't met up over there, Conrad. It would have made it easier for her, coming out here and already knowing you.'

Irresistibly Conrad's and Christabel's eyes met, disentangled. He said, hurriedly, 'I did call, but I missed her. Her neighbour told me she was away on a tour. South-west counties, wasn't it, Christabel?'

'It was. Positively enchanting. And the weather was lovely. It was a magnificent tour altogether. Except for the last day when deterioration set in.' Her eyes flicked to his again, then slid away.

Mary said, 'Oh, you did a trip like that, too, didn't you, Conrad? What a pity it hadn't been the same one. I remember you sending me a card from Lynmouth. You said it was an ideal trip in weather, company, everything. We were so surprised to see you'd taken a tour, we thought you were more likely to have hired a car.'

He said smoothly, 'Oh, I had that idea, but you see far more when you're not driving yourself, especially in the narrow lanes of Devon, or the coast roads of Cornwall.'

Christabel was sorry to see the Macandrews go, but they had given her fresh hope for the future. As she said goodbye to them she said, 'I'll just drop them off in the morning. I want to get back here to help Jonsy, and anyway, school hours mustn't be sabotaged with social calls. I'll meet your people when I pick them up, Ninian.'

She slept well that night.

CHAPTER SEVEN

HEAT from a brazen sky blazed down on them the next day, making that beautiful world of snow and glacier and torrent seem even more like a backdrop to a film scene.

The reality lay in work, with the men from the cottages and Conrad from the homestead out from early light and away. Christabel dropped the children at Mount Hebron, wasted no time there, then returned. She was in old faded jeans today, something she had packed just in case she was allowed to help, and had a loose top in pale blue above it, short-sleeved and low-necked. She had blue and white canvas shoes on her feet.

She had seen Jonsy making huge batches of pikelets and scones before she left and on return found her spreading raspberry and strawberry jam on them, and had a stack of sliced bread ready to be buttered for sandwiches. 'That can be my job, making these,' said Christabel, seizing a knife and a basin of butter. Jonsy had already sliced up cold mutton and beef, had pickle there and lettuce leaves cool and crisp. 'I take it these are for their lunches?'

Jonsy grinned. 'No, for their smokos. They've been going since breakfast and that's nearly four hours ago. They had it at six. They're coming in for their lunch at one. The two married ones will go to their own places, and Gerry Meekham eats with the Greens, but while you were away two extras arrived from Twizel. We want to get the late hay in while the weather lasts. The two casual workers will eat here. You can come with me in the farm truck to hand these out.'

'If you told me where, could I do it alone and let you get on with the lunch?'

'It'd be hard to explain where they are. It's a track rougher than you'll ever have seen. I'll drive, you can open the gates and we'll have ours with the men. That'll mean you'll have some idea of the track and you could take the afternoon lot up, and I'll put my feet up. I don't mind admitting that when Nat's away, like he is now, my feet nearly kill me at the end of the day. He's helping out a nephew of his on a North Island dairy farm just now.'

'I'm so glad to be of use,' said Christabel sincerely.

A huge teapot in a sheepskin-lined circular basket was packed in, and flasks of boiling water and tea-bags. Milk and ice-cold drinks went in a thermo bag. They were carefully stowed in cartons in the back of the battered-looking farm truck.

Jonsy handled the truck as if she'd been doing it all her life. She showed Christabel the ins and outs of it. The track had been just roughly gouged out with a bulldozer at its farther end, and topped with crushed rocks from the estate. The paddocks it went through were immense ones, and some had cattle-stops set in instead of gates, so there weren't too many stops. Christabel was glad of the old-looking jeans. Anything else would have marked her as a greenhorn.

The mountain wind blew the golden-brown hair back from her ears, the air was as fresh as Eden, and in the cloudless sky larks sang as blithesomely and cumberlessly as James Hogg's skylark above the Border Hills. She said so. 'Aye,' said Jonsy, 'and I'm glad you made it Hogg's. I've aye liked his skylark more than Shelley's. It suits here . . . bird of the wilderness. And this *was* a wilderness, even as it says in the memorials in the Cave church. Conrad took you to see that, he tells me.'

'Yes . . . it got to me. To think Catherine and Andrew Burnett could come here—well, across that lake, and carve a home out of surroundings like that, so pitifully far from all they'd known hitherto, yet Lisa, with a maca-dam road a mile from her door, telephone and television, couldn't take it! I feel as if she vandalised the beauty of existence up here for everyone. Enough to put all people who belong here against others who come—and have it easy!'

Jonsy's weatherbeaten hand left the wheel and patted

her knee. 'Don't take it so hard, lass. The pioneers were incomers once. No doubt at times they railed against the conditions, wondered why they'd ever come. And plenty who weren't quite pioneers, but followed in their footsteps, found it too tough. They must have suffered shocking homesickness, and could do nothing about it. There wasn't the money or the quick means of travel then.

'But they found great compensation in their labours . . . once their trees began to grow, their pastures to green up, because in the Mackenzie country man really embellished the work of Nature. They're still doing so . . . the people of today. Look at Lake Benmore, for instance, the man-made hydro lake. It's beyond Twizel, towards Oamaru. You'll get to know it all in time. That lake created beauty where before there was just yellow tussock and now it's a sheet of glimmering blue, and all about it pine and larch and Douglas fir. And let me tell you this . . . I think you're going to suit the Mackenzie . . . this corner of it, anyway. You've got what it takes. Facing us here, after what had happened, took grit.'

So it was that when they drove up to the cluster of men, gathering as they heard the truck, Christabel's eyes were shining. It was an idyllic scene. There was a corner of aspen poplars here, a-quiver in the sun. They dropped down in their shade, gratefully.

The two young men from Twizel made to sit one each side of Christabel, as she knelt to unwrap the sandwiches. One cocked an eye at Conrad, 'If you needed an incentive, boss, to get us here, you could have mentioned the glamorous service . . . in fact, I know of half a dozen chaps who would have fallen over themselves to get here.'

Christabel laughed. 'Yes, I guess there'd be a queue for grub like this! I thought Mrs Johnson must be expecting an army on field manoeuvres.'

The other man, Shaun, burst out laughing. 'One in the eye for you, Bluey. This is the kind of girl who likes obvious compliments—she doesn't recognise the others. Sweetie, he meant you. Like a lush barmaid, drawing in custom.'

Christabel boggled. 'Good grief! I don't think the comparison's good . . . I'm covered in dust and my hair's on end. Aren't these pikelets gorgeous? Though I'd call them drop scones back home, or Scotch pancakes up north. Oh, dear, if I eat like this I'll be like ten-ton Tessie in no time!' She looked up to catch Conrad's eye upon her. Sensitively, she felt he didn't like the men's admiration of her. Anger rose in her breast. He was determined to see her as Lisa's sister. Oh, to the dickens with the man!

He was standing out of the circle of shade, clad only in old denim shorts, his skin so brown his hair looked bleached against it, eyes vividly blue, his body lean yet muscular . . . the sun caught the golden glint of hairs on his shoulders, his chest, gave him a ruddy look. He was every inch a Norseman. Christabel had never been so physically aware of any man, she thought. She clamped down on her thoughts. Physical attraction was important, but wasn't enough. That was how Rogan had brought such disaster upon his life. He'd fallen for Lisa's beauty, the appealing charm that was only a veneer over appalling self-centredness. You needed more than that, for a lifetime.

Jonsy would have lingered longer, but Christabel was having none of that. She wanted no snide remarks on looking on this as a picnic. She got the crocks packed up and slipped into the driving seat. 'Come on, Jonsy . . . I want a lesson so I begin to save you time.'

By the time the men got in at one, they'd had a ring from Mount Hebron to say Ninian had to call at Mount Cook Village to pick something up from the airfield, so would drop the children off on his way.

The men scrubbed up and sat down. Christabel realised there would be great satisfaction in cooking for appetites like this. That over and the dishes stacked away, Jonsy made some huge rhubarb pies. 'I'm sending a couple of these over to Greens'—Sandra's expecting her third and it'll help her out. I wanted these done before I put the roast in. I'll get you to take the pies over, it'll give you a chance to meet Sandra. Better call at Blackwells' cottage too and meet Tania, then you'll have met everyone. But go down to the gate first and collect the mail, then you can deliver theirs to the cottages. It'll save Ninian. If he sees the mail's gone, he'll probably drop the children at the Portals.

'By the time you're back I'll have the afternoon smoko ready. No sandwiches, just the rest of the scones and hunks of fruit cake. By the way,' she added, 'I don't always start from scratch with fresh scones. I stock up the deep freezers in quiet times for shearing and lambing—but I knew you'd be here and would be helping, so I had time today. I'm telling you these things in case I'm away any time in the months to come, and you take over. I wrap the frozen ones in foil and pop them in the oven.'

In the months to come! Oh, bless Jonsy, she was making her feel welcome. If only everyone felt so warmly towards her!

It was a glorious day, with the milky turquoise of the lake ruffled with a feathering breeze and the sun glinting down on the white and red of the tourist helicopter as it rose from its pad at Glentanner Station nearer the head of the lake on its shining-winged flight to show people from the ends of the earth, the glittering and awesome grandeur of range upon range of the Alps and the sweep of the Tasman Sea on the other side, beyond which lay Australia ... how strange to think of an immense island continent just over three hours' air journey away. A place of huge sophisticated cities, ultramarine seas, tumbling surf, orange groves, trackless and pitiless deserts, crocodiles, camels, and sheep and cattle stations so large that they dwarfed these here and reckoned them in square miles! A new world. Enchantment touched Christabel, freeing her heart a little from the frozen ache that had engulfed her ever since Conrad's letter to London had told her Lisa had deserted.

What a huge mail! She flung the bag on the back seat. She'd sort it out at Sandra Green's. As she drove through the Portals, the two great shoulders of hill west and east that almost met, allowing only for the creek-bed and the homestead access, and glimpsed the green oasis of the station property through it, set round the valley, she realised afresh that it was a small kingdom all its own.

Sandra was delighted to see her, but aware she mustn't detain Christabel too long. 'Come back again when the men are working round here and you won't have their smokos to cart to them. Jonsy's already told me *you're* the right sort for here. She needs someone like you just now. Too bad Nat was away when all this happened. But his nephew's need was the greater. He broke his leg and he's got a huge dairy herd. We've just had one emergency after another. I'm thankful my event's far enough off as yet. You'll call on Tania, won't you? Oh, of course, there's mail there for her. She's a grand sort, Jonsy's type but much younger.'

She paused in the sorting. 'Oh, fancy, an airmail parcel from London for Conrad. Oh, help, it's from his publishers and it's marked Urgent. Poor Conrad! I hope it's nothing that'll mean a lot of work for him. He's got enough on his plate as it is. It's exciting, isn't it, him turning out to be an author? He kept it quiet for ages.'

Christabel pulled a face over it. 'I've a feeling this will turn out to be proofs. It'll be for urgent return, *after* correction . . . not something you can really fly through. If he's like my father was—he was an author too—he'll do them twice over and even if he's a speedy reader, it can mean two full days' work at best, more if there are any vital mistakes or alterations. I'd better collect the smokos as soon as I give Tania her mail and let him see them.'

The men had great black rims about their eyes now from the dust of the harvest paddocks, mingled with sweat, and they came quickly to the shade of the trees. Christabel thought it wise to let Conrad drink great draughts of refreshing tea and have some food to replace the energy lost in the last few hours before she told him. She went across to the truck, fished out the parcel, and dropped down beside him on the grass.

'Conrad, I recognised something in the mail. It's from your publishers and marked Urgent, so it's almost bound to be proofs. I thought I ought to bring them to you right away, though——'

'Though you're not sure if I can break off nor not. You're damn right. It's unthinkable. I don't like this long-range forecast. We could get this in if the sou'west change doesn't come as early as they think. Those fellows from Twizel are proving trumps. But——' He slit it open, drew out the long galley-pulls, read the letter, turned the package over, gazed at the postmark and said, 'You wouldn't read about it! I get these in five days as a rule, even up here. This has taken nine. That worsens it. They had a hitch. The proofs should have reached the publishers from the printers sooner. Oh, the gremlins that haunt printing works and post offices! What the blazes am I going to do? Talk about a conflict of loyalties!'

Christabel said diffidently, 'I know only the author can note some mistakes ... like slip-ups in characters' names, sometimes a transposition of paragraphs, but a lot of it's simple enough, merely misprints. Three times I've done the first correcting of proofs for my father's books. He always did the final one, but it saved him much time on the routine stuff. You mightn't like the idea ... some authors hate anyone else going over their work at this stage, but I'd give it a go if it would cut the hours down for you. But I won't be offended if you turn me down. Oddly enough, that's the same firm my father published with, so I know their style.'

For the first time, even though his face was streaked with grime and sweat, and his hair dulled with dust, Conrad Josefsen looked like the Tod Hurst Christabel met and liked ... travelled with, fallen in love with ... he looked open and uncomplicated and extremely thankful.

'Would you, Christabel? Would you really? That's a very sporting offer and I'm in no position to turn it down. It'd be one helluva relief. Could you go back, tell Jonsy she's on her own with the house chores, arrange with the children not to interrupt you, go up to my room, isolate yourself and get right on to it? The carbon copy is in the top drawer of the bigger steel file ... labelled. We're working on till six-thirty. I'll start in on chapter one right after you, when I come up. If I'm just looking for constructional mistakes, and there are rarely many of those, I'll be able to get on with real speed.'

'Done,' said Christabel, getting up, putting the package back in the mailbag so no dust could settle on it, and beginning to pack up the smoko gear. She heard the whirr of the fork-lift starting up as she drove off.

She hadn't been in his room till now. Immediately she felt back in the sort of atmosphere that had prevailed in their own home before she moved to a flat. Dad's writing-room had been like this, also her bedroom, which she had used as a study. Only in hers, of necessity her bed had been there. In this, Conrad's bed was in a small porch off it, something that had obviously been added on for this, and the view from it was breathtaking. When lying in bed he would see the peaks of Mount Cook. Today their triple heights were scarfed with iridescent mist, and a bar of cloud lay across Mount Sefton's ice-face. Was the weather coming sooner?

Christabel came back into the inner room. That window looked out beyond the Portals, to the tussock-tawny slopes of the great hills over-lake, but his desk wasn't under that window, tempting though it must have been to place it there. It would be too distracting. A seasoned author would know that. It was in the middle of the floor and workmanlike rather than ornamental. Back to back with it was a table of matching size, also plain, with stacks of typing paper neatly laid out, some coloured, which she guessed Conrad used for his rough copies, so as not to mix them, boxes of carbon, typing ribbons, paper clips, and piles of memo pads. You wouldn't dare run out of such things, miles from anywhere.

There was a long trough of the books he would use most—Maori dictionaries, books on birds, trees, a history of surnames, a volume of Christian names, foreign phrase-books, and notebooks. Two walls were lined with bookshelves, against others stood steel files and cabinets. They were well labelled. An orderly mind. Conrad must have come home from time to time to work on a book.

Christabel found the first few pages hard going because the story was so fascinating, leaping into action, she had to force her mind, trained and all as it was, to concentrate on looking for errors. Then she steadied and habit took over. When she heard the children arrive she went down, chatted with them for five minutes about their day, impressed upon them that this was an emergency, that they weren't to bother Jonsy too much. Hughie went off to feed the poultry, Davina began to peel potatoes. Christabel hesitated, then said to Jonsy, 'Would there be any chance at dinner time of having Davina bring mine on a tray? I'd like to get on far enough in the story for Conrad not to be waiting for me. You see, I'll be doing the greater part of the marginal correcting, and my pace will be slower than his.'

'Of course—that's sensible. My, but I hope that lad knows how lucky he is to have someone used to that sort of thing, right on the spot.'

By five-thirty she found a hideous mistake . . . surely she'd read exactly those sentences a page or two back? She nearly went zombie-eyed from concentration, but finally reverted to the carbon copy and found out how it had occurred. Two pages of that, with three pages between, had actually run on, with devilish accuracy, and foxed the printer completely. She began making a detailed note. That would lessen Conrad's work. But it made the urgency more vital. He must get this back to London on time.

She got up, a little stiffly, took a turn or two about the room, walked into the sleeping-porch to look at that elegant mountain for inspiration. It wasn't to be seen: It was completely blotted out, yet here, across the whole valley, sunlight lay in a wash of gold and no cloud flecked the blue.

Christabel came back, the work flowed on. There were few errors bar that big one. She heard Conrad's step on the stairs. 'I think you'd better have a break . . . not have your dinner here on a tray. My sainted Aunt Jemima, have you really got as far as that?' he exclaimed.

'Yes, you see I'm an express reader. But I can't guarantee you won't pick up a few mistakes I've missed.'

'Well, for sure. I always pick up some on my second time round, but this is fantastic. How have you found it for error?'

'Very little. Mind you, there might be something only the

author would notice, but apart from one big mistake, repeating one page twice, nothing drastic. I've noted that and got it sorted. You had one mistake yourself, you put midday instead of midnight and I nearly missed it. No, quite definitely I'm not coming down. It's too easy to slow up.'

'Right, I dare not quarrel with that. The men are going back till darkness falls, about eight-thirty at present. I'll shower, then be with you.'

'Right, off you go.'

Conrad turned at the door, said, 'That's summary dismissal.'

Christabel grinned back. 'It was meant to be. Time is precious.'

He came back in a surprisingly short time, bearing a tray of coffee, biscuits, cheeses. 'Come on out to my porch for this. Can't have my secretary fainting for lack of rest. I'd like you to see the peculiar effect of the sunset lighting up Aorangi behind the mist.'

They sat on the edge of his bed and marvelled. Christabel said, 'You'll have seen it like that before?'

'Scores of times ... but it never loses its fascination. You can't capture it on canvas. But weather is coming.' They came back to the inner room. She vacated her chair for him and took one at the table opposite, where she had cleared space among the piles of typing paper. 'I've got that far. Just ask me anything you aren't sure of. I do hope I've not altered anything I shouldn't have altered.'

'Not to worry. I do that too hastily sometimes and have to put "stet" beside it. I've an idea you'll be more proficient than I am, even if my grandfather did make me do a stint as a very junior copyholder, then reader, during varsity holidays. Then I went on to the reporting staff. You'd have liked old Thaddeus, despite his name!'

Their shared spontaneous chuckle did much to dispel their awkwardness with each other. Christabel realised Conrad was working very rapidly, and that only once or twice did he have to add extra proof signs. That pleased her. Time flew, so did the pages. The children came in and kissed them goodnight, Jonsy watching approvingly from the doorway. 'They've been good, so I gave them half an hour's extra viewing time. Right . . .'

At ten-thirty she brought them tea and cookies. 'I'm going off now. An early night will be good, even if breakfast will be later tomorrow.'

Conrad raised a bleached eyebrow. 'How come? I told Bluey and Shaun to be early. I want to beat that weather.'

Jonsy said drily, 'I suggest you look out of your bedroom window.'

Christabel got up too, and all three went into the porch. There, beyond the shoulder of the hill eastward, great swathes of light cut through the darkness, and, opening the windows, the hum of machinery came to them. 'They're working by tractor light, bless them. That could make a big difference,' said Conrad. 'Christabel, you must be horribly stiff, I know I am. I'm getting sleepy, confound it. Let's go on up and see them. Take some flasks up. Think of the letters you'll write to your London friends, about harvesting by moonlight, among the mountains!'

Christabel expected Jonsy to say this was clean crazy, but she just said, 'Yes, awa' wi' you. Nothing like the night air in these altitudes. By the way, the boys from Twizel are staying here. They're not going on home when they finish.'

Christabel looked longingly at the balance of the three-page pulls. 'I'll only go if we come back to work on these again when we're refreshed.'

Conrad Thaddeus Brockenhurst Josefsen was in high gig. 'I've got myself a slavedriver in this girl! Bosses are supposed to crack the whip, not employees.'

'Ah, but I'm not an employee, and you've got to kow-tow to voluntary workers.'

'You soon will be an employee—make no mistake about that. From mid-afternoon today, you're on the payroll.'

They filled the flasks, then Conrad said, 'These are going in the bags on the trail-bike, and you're going on the pillion. You'll have to hang on tightly. They're going back and forth to the shed all the time and I don't want to meet that loader on the track with a wider vehicle.'

As they jolted over the stones Christabel had a most unreal feeling. Surely this couldn't be happening? If anyone had told her that disillusioning time she had rung that boarding-house and was told no one of that name had ever stayed there, that in less than eight months' time she would be jolting over glacial rocks crushed to a semblance of a surface, under an Alpine moon in the South Pacific, with the man she was endeavouring to trace, and they would be harvesting in immense paddocks, on a hot February night, she'd have thought they were mad.

She thought of another summer night, on St Catherine's Hill above Winchester ... and knew a swift nostalgia ... then she had fully trusted that man known as Tod Hurst, a man who had kissed her in a way no other man had ever done, and she had responded in a way she had never wanted to respond before ... don't soften too much towards him, Christabel, you have to stay here because of the children. Make yourself useful to him, yes, but don't fall for him again, ever.

She was surprised to find the flasks intact, but discovered they had been inserted into padded casing. The men were glad to see them. Bluey said, 'Wish I'd taken up journalism myself ... you've sure got the best of it, Conrad, with company like this. Me, I was never a lucky guy ... I've got to put up with this lot, all male.'

Just as they mounted the bike to return Conrad said, looking back towards the Alps, 'Ever see anything to equal that?'

It had an ethereal quality, silvery light stretching palely away from them to the sable shadows of foothills rising out of deep, ghostly valleys. There was enough starshine and moonlight to catch the chiffon-like drifts of cloud moving against the dark-blue sky, and faint and far away, a pearly shimmer that must be a radiance on the bosom of the lake.

Suddenly it was all too heady, too romantic for Christabel. A wind that had been too warm a moment ago shifted and she felt for the first time the reality of the ice and snow such a short distance away. 'Let's get back to warmth and shelter,' she said, and shivered.

Conrad kicked the engine into noise that desecrated the Alpine stillness, and behind them the machines roared to life again.

As they entered the house he said, 'Nearly midnight. You'll be dead tomorrow, let's call it a day.'

She looked at him squarely. 'Are *you* going to bed?'

'No—my mind is far too active now. I'll have to work it off.'

'So is mine. Let's at it.'

It was three-thirty when they heard the machines being driven in, and on the stilly air the closing of the doors in the cottages, and the sounds of Bluey and Shaun going into the shearing quarters. At five to four Christabel handed over the last chapter to Conrad. 'You're off?' he asked.

'I can't,' she said simply and with finality. 'I want to see you finish it. Don't ask me to go.'

He accepted that, bent over his task. So it was nearly five when he finally laid aside his ballpoint. He raised his head and looked at her, sitting so still, so close to him, just across the table backed to his desk. She said, as one stating a fact, 'It's good, that last chapter, isn't it?'

He said, 'I hoped so. I'm not one who likes too many ends left undone. I like conclusion. I don't much care for the bleats about it being more artistic otherwise. In the main, if people are worth while, they achieve some sort of lasting happiness, even if it's not always handed to them on a platter, don't you think?' He paused, then added, 'Don't be frightened to disagree.'

'Yes, I think mostly they do. At least the people I like to wr—like to read about, do.' Heavens, she'd nearly said write about! She didn't know why she was reluctant to tell Conrad she also wrote. Time enough when her first book came out. This man was a professional by now; she was just a beginner.

He nodded. 'I know this was a task you were just

racing through, but what did you think of the way those two people acted—I mean the way they resolved their problem? It was tricky, keeping that thread surviving through the other adventures of the thriller, but I wanted it to come through. Oh, I'm not putting it very well, but I'd really value your opinion on this. *Would* those two have behaved ... well ... so nobly, for want of a better word? Is it realistic enough? Would they have renounced that chance, feeling as they did?'

In the strong light over his desk her eyes were almost wholly green and very knowledgeable. 'I think you mean, don't you, that in most books of this nature, they'd have hopped into bed with each other, seeing he wasn't free? But they turned their backs on that and in the end it brought them to much greater happiness—though not with each other. You also mean that some might say that, human nature being what it is, they'd have succumbed long before—especially in the situation they were in. Extreme danger, close quarters and so on. That they could have been excused since they both knew they might never get out of it alive?'

'I do mean that. But how did it strike you? Credible ... that they didn't?' His eyes were intent on hers, and brilliant. Christabel said slowly, 'Yes. Because they were such fine individuals that it would have taken away from them, somehow. Sometimes I hate that phrase: it's only human nature after all, because even in my short life I've seen humans do incredibly noble things. If that chapter, nine, wasn't it? had gone the other way, something would have gone out of that book for me. I liked the fact that he returned to save his marriage. They showed their humanness in the way they had to struggle against succumbing. There's no disgrace in being tempted. It's how you meet the temptation that counts. And it can make you more understanding of the ones who do succumb. No casting of stones. These folk met the challenge and overcame it. I had a feeling it might help other people, readers, to do the same. Oh, I *liked* it, Conrad, I liked it very much! I had to go back over that whole chapter, because I got so engrossed in it, I wasn't sure I'd picked up all the misprints.'

He stood up, came round to her, pulled her to her feet by her hands. 'Good girl! Good girl. You've really done something for me, bless you. You've given me courage to go on.'

Christabel blinked at his intensity. 'You mean ... oh, you can't mean you were thinking about not going on writing? That would be a crime!'

He laughed and it seemed to her it was a strange laugh. Almost exultant, as if he had just come through some highly emotional experience. He shook his head. A thick lock of fair hair fell over his brow and he shook it back again. 'No, not that. You ... just resolved something for me, that's all.'

'I did? How very peculiar! Look, Conrad, you're almost on an emotional high, sort of exhilarated about getting a tremendous and well-nigh impossible task done. You must go to bed. I think the dawn is beginning to streak the sky. Tomorrow morning this wad of proofs can be parcelled up and perhaps I could take it to the village. It'll go down from there by air, won't it?'

'Yes, then off from one of the international airports. Seeing the proofs took longer than usual to reach me. I'm going to ring London tomorrow at eleven in case of another delay in their return. I'll tell them to check their copy closely where that page gets repeated. I'm immensely grateful. *And I meant what I said about the pay-roll.*'

She pulled her hands away, said passionately, 'I *won't* be paid. You can't put a price on everything. I *won't*. I was glad to do it. We may have had our differences, but at least I appreciate that you're doing a big job ... two big jobs——'

'*Pax*, girl! I didn't mean payment for this. I've realised—after all—that I'm fortunate you revolted against my ban against you coming. I don't want the regularity of my book production to drop too much, but I can see months ahead devoted largely to Thunder Ridge. I must do that, for Rogan's sake. But though I've always done even the final copy myself till now, I believe I could so prepare future ones for publication that you could type them for me. Would you?'

Suddenly she was fighting tears and walked over to the window to hide it from him. But her voice, shaking, gave her away. 'I would—I—haven't known quite what to do. I felt I must stay near the children. I—spoke to Mary about this. She thought I might be able to get a job at one of the accommodation places in the village. So th-thank you.'

Conrad strode across the room to her, put an arm across her shoulders. It was comforting and warm through her thin silk blouse. He gave her a hug. 'You could have been on the payroll without that, silly nit. For the way you seem prepared to help Jonsy. But this might boost your ego more—the job no one else could possibly do. Cheer up, you're utterly weary. Like you said, the dawn's coming up. Come and see it from the porch window. It fingers the ice-face of Sefton first.'

It was quite a superlative moment. An incredible one, too. Here she was, with Tod Hurst—Thaddeus Brockenhurst—Conrad Josefsen, the man who had first enchanted her, then repelled her, who had completely dismayed her on Timaru railway station, and had made her pilgrimage to comfort her sister's children all but impossible. Now—could she really credit it?—she was on his payroll, secretary to him as an author and watching the dawn with him, to boot!

Here it was. The rising sun that would be a ball of fire mounting the horizon of the Pacific Ocean a hundred miles to the east, here pierced the thin veil of mist that still obscured Aorangi slightly, and it was just like seeing a rainbow dissolve into a fabric of colours more vivid than mother-of-pearl, and though one knew it would be evanescent, it would remain in the memory for ever.

Conrad said, 'Isn't it strange? We're actually seeing Mount Cook through a sort of prism of light . . . cloud and mist are such enemies to safety here . . . we're always aware of that . . . but somehow at this moment it's adding even more beauty to a scene that seemed superlative even without the mist. Oh, look, those rays are shifting, and the mountain is disappearing from sight. We may be the only two in the world to see that, this morning. Go to bed, Christabel, Jonsy won't waken us a moment before she must. It would be silly to say goodnight when dawn's breaking, so I'll just say pleasant dreams to you. You deserve them.'

She turned at the door, said what she hadn't meant to say. 'So do you, Thaddeus Brockenhurst, author. You deserve it for that ninth chapter you didn't spoil.'

He gave her a long unsmiling look . . . almost a searching look, then just nodded and turned back to his window. She closed his door softly and tiptoed to her bed. She slept dreamlessly, after all, for three hours, and woke like a giant refreshed, heard the clink of dishes downstairs, slipped on a housecoat of velvety lavender and went downstairs.

Conrad was at the table in his workaday khaki shorts and a blue cotton vest, freshly showered, the fair hair slicked wetly back.

Jonsy, turning from the stove with the porridge-pot, said, 'We weren't going to waken you. You needn't have come down. Conrad's taking the children to Mount Hebron, they're just getting ready.'

'He isn't, you know. Conrad is going out with the men to get the last paddock of hay in. Taking the children to school is my job. I'm now on the payroll, partly as Thaddeus Brockenhurst's secretary, partly as general rouseabout, and I must earn my keep.'

Conrad, surprisingly, made no objections. Christabel added, 'On my return I'll pick up those proofs, if you wrap and address them before I come back, Conrad.'

'Things this morning,' said Jonsy, 'seem to be on a very good footing.'

Christabel thought so too, and pushed any lingering doubts to the back of her mind.

CHAPTER EIGHT

CHRISTABEL found the twenty-five miles to Mount Cook ... or thirty-two kilometres as the signpost said, all too short. How could it be otherwise with a tantalising view like that spread before one ... a fairy-like mountain that dominated the view one moment and the next disappeared behind diaphanous gossamer mist? There were massive shoulders of hills, grey and tawny, crouching in front and seeming so enormous in themselves one could only imagine the height of the king of these Alps when one got closer. The gleaming mass of the Tasman Glacier gave the illusion of a horrific river suddenly turned by a wizard's hand into incredible depths of solid ice.

The lake shimmered under hot sunshine. It didn't seem possible that last night the men had worked right through because they were afraid of a break in the weather. The road veered left and here was the Alpine village. It was all in keeping with the spirit of the mountains, buildings of oiled wood and natural stone, chalets showing peaked roofs among pines and gums, gardens reminiscent of the bright gardens of Austria and Switzerland that Christabel remembered, the scarlets and pinks of geraniums splashing and cascading in a riot of colour, golds and whites of huge daisies and the paler alpine plants and creepers in myriads.

The Glencoe Motor Inn spread itself out against a rugged mountainside that was clothed with native bush, where signposts pointed out walking tracks winding upwards into what should prove a fairyland, where gnarled and twisted trunks green with mosses and ferns made one feel it was a setting for a Walt Disney film. If a little spotted fawn had strayed down from the bush, it would have seemed the most natural thing to meet.

Mount Sefton must present its implacable barrier just round that bend, but she must get this away first. Ah, here was a sign to the post office. It was built in keeping with all the other places. Christabel felt a little nervous. This was her first contact with the tourist service people since arriving, and Lisa's dramatic end, with a well-known visitor here, had been so very public. She tightened her lips and went in.

The parcel was, of course, very clearly marked with a publisher's address and detailed: 'Printed matter only,' and 'Sender: Thaddeus Brockenhurst (Conrad Josefsen), Thunder Ridge Station, Mount Cook, New Zealand.' Evidently his identity was no longer a secret.

The girl was so pleasant, so friendly. 'Oh, how gorgeous—tell me, is this another book from my favourite author?'

Christabel met it with a matching cordiality. 'In a manner of speaking, yes. Not a manuscript hot from the typewriter, but the corrected proofs of the next book to come.'

'Oh, splendid. It's a pity it takes three or four months to reach the shops. It seems so odd that airmail is so quick, now, and surface mail so horribly slow—fewer and fewer ships. Yet my grandmother tells me that when she came out here in the 1920s she used to get mail with unvarying regularity every five weeks. Makes me feel we progress in one direction and slip back in the other.'

Christabel nodded. 'Yes. It's a topsy-turvy world. I was in London just a fortnight or so ago, yet spent time with an aunt in Vancouver on the way, and I've been at Thunder Ridge some time now. I'm a half-sister to the late Mrs Rogan Josefsen and I've come out to look after her children.' No one could have guessed what it had cost her to come out with that, but she felt it was the best way.

The girl responded immediately. 'Well, what a sport you are. That'll help Mrs Johnson out. How is Rogan?'

'Coming along, but it'll be a long convalescence.'

'Well, with Conrad holding the fort, he'll not need to

rush back home. He's better in Timaru with his parents. I hope you like it here. Might you stay? Or will you miss London too much?'

'Too early to say yet, about staying, I mean. But oddly, I haven't been homesick. I'll stay as long as they need me.'

'Have you explored the village yet? It's very pretty . . . and teeming with life. You could park your car in front of the Hermitage and wander round. Or at the Park Headquarters.'

'Is it a little park all to itself?' asked Christabel. 'Where would I find it?'

The girl chuckled. 'The Park I mean is the Mount Cook National Park, and it covers about seventy thousand hectares, and takes in all the most spectacular peaks of the Alps. Over a third of it's permanent snow and ice. The Headquarters building is the information point—a lovely building.'

Conrad had said, 'Don't hurry back, you've earned a break.' Trampers and climbers were everywhere. They had bright anoraks on and heavy packs. The holiday-makers who weren't making for the heights were in sun-frocks and shorts, beautifully tanned, carefree, laughing, some emerging from the Youth Hostel and the motels. All the houses, she had been told by Jonsy, belonged to the tourist sector, occupied by guides, rangers, or staff of the two huge hotels, Glencoe and the Hermitage, or the various people who serviced the area.

Christabel stopped entranced at the sight of the Her-mitage as she swung the car round below the huge bank where creepers tumbled down the boulders, and up to the car park. It was so wide, with immense scenic windows, a kiosk-like structure at one end that was the private bar, and at the other a public bar, a souvenir shop, a coffee-shop, all designed in mountain style. She went in, ordered a coffee and a pastry and relaxed. When she was finished she moved into the souvenir shop and was caught up, immediately, into a cosmopolitan atmosphere, with the sound of many languages catching her ear, reminding her of the tours of Europe she had taken, with her parents. Others, though, reminded her that she was now in South Pacific, especially a group whose tour leader had persuaded them to wear name-tags, with the country of their origin inscribed Samoan, Fijian, Rarotongan, Tahitian. Christabel liked it.

She bought some cards for neighbours, and for Tim and Janice, and went out through the lobby of the hotel. This could be any luxury inn anywhere and it breathed money, adventure, elegance. She could imagine Lisa adoring it. If only she had been content with visiting here with Rogan for dine-and-dances, not wanting it all the time and finally falling for all Burford Grosset had promised her in glamorous Hong Kong.

She walked out briskly, suddenly wanting, with urgency, Thunder Ridge, the lonely valley with its portals that shut it in, to be back in the big working kitchen, to the constant demands upon her time; she wanted the bleating of sheep, the sun shining on the flanks of chestnut Herefords, the song of the creek over the glacial stones that were so ancient they spoke of eternal values.

She walked into the kitchen half an hour later, said gaily, 'Here I am!' to Jonsy who was taking an outsized pasty out of the oven and who said as she put it on the cooling grid on the marble slab, 'Well, lass, how did you find the village?'

'Very pretty, very exciting . . . I suppose. Half a dozen languages going full tilt in the souvenir shop and a very friendly girl in the post office, a great admirer of Thaddeus Brockenhurst, but oh, how glad I am to be back home!'

A small sound made her turn in the direction of the far door. Conrad stood there. 'Why?' he asked.

It seemed an abrupt, even disbelieving question, yet this time it didn't throw Christabel at all. She laughed, shrugged her shoulders, said, 'It's so ridiculous when I'm London-born and bred, but after a few days here, shut into this valley by the Portals, I suddenly felt crowded in when I was picking out a few souvenirs for the folk back there. I wanted to be back here. Oh, it's quite absurd. Jonsy, what can I do for you?'

'Set the table, Christie. They're coming in for lunch a bit earlier, Conrad says.'

She flung the cloth on the table, opened a drawer for cutlery, said, 'Tell me, Conrad, did you get your publisher? I suppose that's what you came back for? To ring him at eleven?'

'No, you nit. You'd better try to remember you're in the Southern Hemisphere, and we're a day—well, twelve hours—ahead of London. Not that I expect to tell my secretary to ring London very often, but my publisher will be in the bosom of his family right now, probably. I'm ringing him at eleven tonight, which with us an hour on, for daylight saving, will be ten in the morning with him.'

Christabel looked abashed. 'I shall never get used to that. It's like being in a time machine.'

Mrs Johnson said, 'I'm just going to get tidied up. I'll be back in a moment.'

That gave Christabel a chance to say something she didn't want to say in front of her. 'Conrad, when the post office clerk remarked that she hoped this was another thriller going away, I realised it's not a secret any longer. I should have tumbled to that when you put your own name in brackets on the packet. Didn't you then take a risk in not letting me know sooner, instead of letting me just find it out for myself on Timaru Station? Your dual personality, I mean. The Dr Jekyll and Mr Hyde business?'

He said calmly, 'Oh, I hope you'll never regard me as a Mr Hyde.'

'That's not answering the question. I said wasn't that a risk?'

'It was too recent to be much of a risk.'

'How recent? Did you suddenly get written up as Thaddeus?'

'Yes. Very sudden. But I gave permission then. I told you my reasons, as a journalist, with the prospect of fellow-journalists having to review my books and not liking to let themselves go, if the reviews had to be adverse. But by now, when it broke, I'd more or less made my reputation.'

'When—and how—did it break?' she asked.

He sighed. 'You've got a persistent streak in you. I don't want to keep harping on this. When reporters arrived here, after Lisa and Burford's accident. One of them had worked for my grandfather, and knew me. That, plus my style of writing. Although he kept the tragedy out of it, my connection with it, I mean, he wrote me up, separately, and published it the next day or two— quite a good article, giving my mixed background, high-country station, and reporter's desk and assignments. It gave my thrillers their setting as authentic, the mountains, the helicopters, glacier-traverse stuff, rescue stunts and so on. All of which have been part of my life for years It was hardly likely you'd see a newspaper days old, between Timaru and Christchurch. And, to be quite candid, when you just about hit me in the solar plexus by announcing per phone that you'd just arrived in Christchurch from London, I was much more concerned about what you were going to say about the Tod Hurst— Conrad Josefsen combination when you met me.'

'Oh, so you *were* worried about that, were you? No one would have guessed.'

'Of course I was. It was a caddish thing to do. A sudden impulse I ought to have throttled at birth—or confessed pronto.'

'Then why didn't you?'

He considered his answer. 'For reasons best known to myself it became apparent to me I'd be better to wait.'

Her lip curled. 'Oh, come. You really don't expect me to believe that? I don't think you ever meant to. And the more time that elapsed, the more impossible it became.'

Conrad took no umbrage. 'Not so, Christabel Windsor. I made up my mind I'd tell you as soon as I called on you in London. But then——'

'But then you found you didn't want to pursue the

acquaintance any further. Fair enough, I warned you that might happen, remember? I even told you I wouldn't mind. But you ought to have owned up to your identity. Why didn't you?'

He drummed his fingers on the table. 'I'd rather not tell you . . . yet.'

Christabel stared. 'That's the last thing I'd have credited you with, then or now—indecision. You just aren't the havering sort. I don't think these things can be postponed. I'd rather know, even if I won't like it.'

'Look, I acted too hastily once and regretted it. If I've had second thoughts now, it's better. Would you leave it at that?'

He met her gaze unflinchingly enough, even though hers was a despising one. The table was between them and antagonism was in the very way they held themselves. They heard Jonsy coming. Christabel said wearily, 'Okay, leave it at that. After all, I've got to work with you, and I hand it to you, it isn't going to be easy keeping the thread of your narrative and managing a place like this.'

Conrad grinned. 'Some of it's so mechanical, I can brood on my story while I'm doing it. I'll miss out on that when I'm busy on the farm papers. But I've got the nerve to imagine you can lessen my work in that department too.'

Shaun and Bluey came in, dispelling all stiffness with their teasing, happy-go-lucky way, and in high spirits in knowing they'd beaten the weather. 'With all of us on that, it's been a bit of cake. Another hour and a half, and we'll have it whacked.'

Jonsy said as she served a delectable steamed pudding, a chocolate sponge mixture with pear quarters embedded in it, 'Oh, I nearly forgot, Christie, some woman rang from Dunedin with a message for you.'

'For *me*? Can't be. I don't know anyone in Dunedin, or anywhere else in New Zealand for that matter. What——'

'Well, you know her son and she thinks he's bound to call on you in the next day or two and wants you to ask him to ring her.'

Christabel positively boggled. 'This is ridiculous! You mean—is he from London? Did I meet him somewhere? I don't remember meeting a Kiwi with a mother in Dunedin. Or even a Kiwi, without knowing about his family. Except C—except Rogan.' She corrected herself just in time. 'Jonsy, I think she got the wrong number. It must have been for someone staying at Mount Hebron, or Glentanner.'

'She said he met you just recently, didn't say where, but she knew you were from London, staying here with relations, and he told his mother he'd drop in to see you. Apparently there's some hitch in his papers for varsity and she wants him to ring home. His——'

'Oh,' light broke on Christabel, 'it must be that boy on the train. Sorry, Jonsy, you were going to say . . .?'

'That his name is Gordon Millon.'

Christabel turned her hands out and shrugged. 'I knew only the last name. He said as he put my luggage out, "Might see you some time, who knows? . . . the name's Millon." But for goodness' sake, it seems a nerve to use us for messages.'

Jonsy was indulgent. 'Not really. Students are casual the world over. Let's hope he turns up soon, the beginning of varsity's not far away.'

'I hope he doesn't show up at all,' said Christabel crossly. 'It's not as if this is *my* home and I can give hospitality to whom I choose.'

'Oh, lass, don't fash yourself about that. We're used to people turning up for a meal or a bed. She sounded a very nice woman.'

Shaun and Bluey were chuckling. Bluey said, 'What is it from Christchurch to Timaru, Shaun? About a hundred miles? Well, for sure our Christie wastes no time. Mows 'em down like ninepins—doesn't give us a chance. We hope he doesn't turn up, too. Look, if he does, and wants you off to the Village with him, to take a turn or two on the dance floor, tell him we asked you first. Can't have you rusticating here, pining for Piccadilly and the Embankment.'

Christabel opened her mouth to say that there was

nothing she felt less like doing than dancing, at the moment, when Conrad cut in. 'Sorry, chaps, I beat you to it. But not tonight. She's tired and so will we be come nightfall. But you can tag along with us some time if you like. But I tell you what—when we finish this job, we're taking the afternoon off. The others know, but they're going to get on with the repairs of the cattle-pens, and take time off with their families, next week. But we're having a swim before that promised weather catches up with us. You're coming too, Jonsy. Time you had a break. When Nat gets back he'll have the hide off me if you look washed out. It's about time we all relaxed after what we've been through this last month.'

There was a splendid swimming hole in the creek, a natural one, dammed up a little to deepen it, clear, cold mountain water that cascaded down from the foothills. Willows fringed it, and one that had tilted over in floodtime, had fallen with its trunk in such a position, it made an excellent diving-board. You could see every pebble on the bottom.

Jonsy was a splendid swimmer. She grinned. 'I had to be, to take care of the four daredevils of youngsters Kate and Ivar produced. They nearly killed me. I had to become almost a mountaineer too. Where they went, I went too.'

Christabel laughed, turned on her back and floated, kicking a foot now and then. This was sheer heaven. For the first time for weeks, the weight seemed gone from round her heart. Life wasn't all battling against prejudice and the knowledge that someone of one's own blood had brought tragedy to this family. It seemed there was time also for play and laughter and new adventures. And she was needed, not only for the children, but her particular skills were in demand here, at the typewriter.

Shaun came up under her feet, seized them, and tipped her back under. She turned in a flash and went after him, catching him off balance. Conrad, poised above them on the tree-trunk, laughed indulgently. He was in blue trunks and the whole scene took on a photo-graphic quality ... blue trunks, bronzed body, fair hair bleached to pale straw by the sun, a sky above him so blue it seemed unreal, and masses of white clouds that looked like churned-up soapsuds. She said so, pointing.

Conrad's blue eyes glinted down on her. 'What a pros-aic description from an author's daughter ... soapsuds! I'm sure you could do better than that. But they won't be white for long, they'll turn inky before the thunder and lightning start. We'd better pile in the truck before long and head for home or we'll be drenched.'

'I don't believe you. Surely night at the earliest.'

'You're a green girl when it comes to mountain wea-ther. Better make the most of the next quarter of an hour.'

As he dived in, she swam to the tree-trunk, clambered up, lay along it like a recumbent lion, Bluey said. Conrad laughed, 'Except that lions don't wear delectable bikinis in purple and green. You don't mean to stay up there, do you, Christabel?'

'I do. Even Jonsy's as brown as a nut. I feel conspicu-ous with all this white skin. But of course I came from winter there to summer here. I'm browner as a rule.'

Conrad swam to the trunk, put his hands up to hold himself against the current and let his legs go underneath it. 'I remember that. I remember how brown your arms were against that sleeveless white dress that night in Win-chester. The beech trees were just on the turn, and I thought you suited the woods—brown hair, brown skin, and eyes neither brown nor green.'

Her face was resting sideways on her outstretched arms and just a few inches from Conrad's. 'Careful! They could have acute hearing. And who wants to remember that night, anyway? Not I for one. I was disillusioned about you too soon after. Off you go, Conrad Josefsen, I'm stay-ing here in the interests of tanning.'

He didn't care, he turned in a flash, swam to the op-posite bank, clambered up, dived in. She turned her face to the other side, not to watch him. Suddenly Jonsy cried, 'Come on, men, come on, Christie, the wind's changing.'

It was dramatic. Through a deep rift in the mountain pattern, a different wind swept through, turning the tussocks on the far hillside to silver instead of gold, as they bent before it. Two horses had taken their stand under some willows in the next paddock and now turned their backs to the sou'west. They looked up at the sky, and the sudsy clouds had massed together, darkening, and the edges where they hadn't quite met were rimmed with molten fire, an eerie effect.

Jonsy and the men were on the bank. Christabel stood up and ran along the horizontal trunk to the edge, they scooped up their towels and made for the truck. Jonsy reached the driver's seat, Christabel scrambled in beside her, Bluey and Shaun went in the tray of the truck. Christabel expected Conrad to follow them, because the cab was really only a two-seater, but he squashed in beside her, to the sound of aggrieved yells from the men.

He said, laughing, to Christabel, 'Shove over, mate,' and put a wet arm round her shoulders to make more room for himself. As Jonsy expertly turned the vehicle on the rough ground, lightning zigzagged across the sky in a dramatic spectacle; they held their breath, the thunder rolled, tossing backwards and forwards among the barriers of mountain on all sides.

It was impossible not to enjoy it. Then, after an ominous pause, the skies opened. The windscreen wipers were quite unable to cope. Buckets of water streamed down the glass. Conrad said, 'Better pull in for a bit, Jonsy.' He chuckled. 'The men can't get any wetter than they were in the pool!'

Christabel turned an indignant face up to him. 'Of all the callous remarks! *You're* sitting here very comfortably while they're——' His eyes, an inch or two from hers, were dancing.

'Not only comfortable, but stirring in them wild envy; the size of this cab, under these conditions, is a bonus! Oh, look, Jonsy, our Miss Windsor is blushing all over her face . . . in fact, I can't see where that blush ends . . .'

'If there was room,' said Miss Windsor, 'I'd smack your face! Jonsy, make him behave!'

Jonsy, laughing, said, 'He was my only failure out of the whole brood. Don't ask me to take him in hand now.'

Conrad said mournfully, 'I'm being maligned. Jonsy has always been able to bring me to heel and well she knows it. She had no inhibitions about sparing the rod . . . I tingle at the thought.'

At which Mrs Johnson leaned over and caught him a stinging slap on his bare thigh. 'Well, tingle with that! And in case Christie thinks I was a martinet, I never used more than my hand, and always aimed for the place ordained for spanking. That one would have been irrepressible without a spanking occasionally.'

'I believe you,' said Christabel. 'And I think the rain is lessening.'

'Spoilsport,' said Conrad. 'I don't mind how long we linger, in circs like these.' Jonsy started up again, and they drove slowly along the track which was, by now, a minor stream. They went over some cattle-stops and struck a better surface. As they pulled up at the house they saw one of the cars from Mount Hebron coming.

'They must have decided to beat the storm,' said Conrad. It drew up behind them. Children piled out and rushed into the house. The men from the truck-tray leapt down and gained shelter. Then the three scantily-clad figures from the cab fell out and rushed to stand on the verandah. The driver of the Mount Hebron car was last.

Conrad gave a yell, said, 'That's Barbara . . . how marvellous!' and leapt towards her and caught her in a great hug. 'Barbie . . . now everything'll be all right.' Then, when he'd kissed her, he seemed to recollect that he had an audience.

Bluey said, 'Well, I'm darned, he gets the best of everything. And we remain chilled to the bone!'

Conrad burst out laughing. 'You two use the showers off the verandah. We'll use the inside ones. That makes it fair, chaps, because I'll have to wait till the women have theirs. Barbie, I've soaked you. Sorry about that, but I'm so glad to have you back.'

Barbara shook herself, said, 'I can tell that. It's awfully good for the ego, Conrad darling, but dampening otherwise.' She looked up at Christabel, turning rapidly goose-fleshed, and said, 'Oh, now I do remember you on the plane. We exchanged that grin, remember, over that woman who was such a trial to the stewards . . . Conrad's parents told me you were on it. Now, rush in, all of you. Jonsy, don't catch cold. Make for that hot bath. I'll greet you properly afterwards.'

The hot water was wonderful. How odd that after re-velling in a mountain stream, for cooling-off purposes, and basking in the sun, now one could turn to shivering. Christabel slipped into her leaf-brown pants, pulled on a white cowl-necked cashmere sweater, rubbed at her short brown hair, ran a comb through it, fluffed it up at the ends, then applied make-up a little more heavily than usual. She stared at herself, wondering why, pulled a face and said to her reflection, 'You idiot . . . what does it matter? He said Barbara was special!' But anyway, make-up was good for the morale.

It was quite evident Barbara was at home here, even if it seemed she'd been away most of the time since Rogan's marriage. She had put a light to the fire, had the kettle boiling, and quite a large afternoon tea set out. It needed to be ample, as she'd brought the three Mac-andrew children along with her. It was quite evident that they adored their older cousin and hadn't wanted to part with her.

'I got a lift up yesterday as far as Tekapo, and stayed the night, then got a lift with a Public Works truck. Ministry of Works, I mean.'

Conrad said, 'You didn't feel you should stay longer at Timaru?'

Christabel saw Jonsy give him a swift, calculating glance. What it meant she didn't know. But it meant something.

Barbara had an easy way with her. 'No, I only stayed at first because I thought your mother and father looked a bit done up. They were tearing backwards and for-wards to hospital . . . you know how it is these days, they're only too pleased to have relations help with feeding. But Rogan's able to use his fingers again, so the pressure's off. I really just kept things going at the house.'

'But you've seen Rogan?'

'Yes, but I didn't overdo. I think only family is necessary at first. Other visitors tire the patient, but he's on the up and up now. I thought I'd better come up and get on with my job. Mary has so many other things to do she helps Gran a lot now because Gran quite unobtrusively does a lot of Grandpa's chores these days. Even if he is a giddy wonder for ninety-seven.'

Christabel's eyes bulged. 'Ninety-seven? Oh, you're having me on! He couldn't be. He was riding round the sheep with Ninian the other day.'

Barbara laughed. 'That's Grandpa! He's years older than Gran. But being married to her would keep anyone young. Anyway, it's time I was home with them and it's ideal if I can teach two families, plus the shepherds' children.'

'It is that,' said Conrad in a tone of deepest satisfaction.

Barbara said quickly, 'Because it brings me back to my mountains.'

'That too,' said Conrad, and Christabel could have sworn Jonsy gave him a warning glance.

Suddenly the comradeship newly experienced with Conrad was overlaid with shadow for Christabel. He had said Barbara was special. She loved the mountains, was born and bred to them. Her people were farming not many miles away and she had always spent a lot of time at Mount Hebron. But something had happened to send Barbara off to Fiji, a place as different from this as it could be. What? Everything will be all right now Barbara is home, Conrad had said.

But Conrad's life, for many years, had been in the newspaper world in Auckland, the city that covered an area like London, even if it had less than a million population. Had Barbara felt she couldn't take that life? Had she fled from New Zealand so she wouldn't be tempted to compromise? But things were changing. Christabel thought of that room of Conrad's, crammed with reference books. Had he, after returning from London, come down to the old homestead, to Jonsy and Nat, to write full-time and to just lend a hand occasionally on the property, satisfying the two sides to his personality? And if that was so, had Barbara decided she could now come home?

Suddenly Christabel thought of something. Had Conrad had it in mind to return to Thunder Ridge, because then Barbara might come home to him? Had he decided to take a trip to London first to see his publisher, and when over there, when he had succumbed to that not very creditable scheme of finding out what Lisa's sister was really like, been surprised to find himself drawn to Christabel?

She found her pulses quickening at the thought. It could have been a genuine attraction. But then why had he changed so suddenly? Overnight? Perhaps that very night, between the sweetness of their caresses and meeting next morning, he must have come to himself, realised Barbara had first place in his heart, and that it was a grave risk, taking another girl from London to the heart of the mountains? Rogan's experiment had not paid off. And Barbara was a true daughter of the misty gorges. Christabel shut out all thoughts like that and went downstairs.

Barbara was lovely, with the same rich brown beauty her grandmother, Elspeth Macandrew, must have had when young. Now Elspeth had snow-white hair, but her brown eyes still sparkled youthfully and she had an enchanting rose in her cheeks that ebbed and flowed. Barbara's colour paled and glowed like that. What dancing eyes she had! She was bubbling over with the joy of being home.

'Oh, yes,' she was telling the boys, 'I loved Fiji, the colour of it, the warm seas, the launch trips—I can't understand why more New Zealanders don't go there. It's so near. But for living . . . for keeps, give me my mountains.'

The warm brown eyes flickered to Conrad's, held for a moment, then looked away. His eyes gave the merest answering flicker of understanding, and despite the cashmere sweater Christabel gave an involuntary shiver. Conrad noticed. 'Cold, or just someone walking over your grave-to-be? Come and sit nearer the fire.' He pulled out a chair. She wished the idea hadn't hit her when so many people were about. She would sort it out later, in the quietness of their evening. The children would be in bed, Barbara and the Mount Hebron children gone. If that had been the reason for Conrad's withdrawal, she could understand it. A man could get carried away and then remember his former loyalty.

There had been a lull in the storm, an uneasy quiet, as if the forces of tempest and cloud were biding their time, then were about to hurl an onslaught against the puny shelters men had dared to build in the wilderness. The room was dark save for the flames of the leaping fire, then it was lit with a light so bright it hurt the eyes, a whiteness unendurable. They all stopped talking and waited, listening for the thunder that would succeed.

Nevertheless, though they feared damage, there was a splendid exultancy in watching such an unparalleled display of the elements. At least Christabel had never before seen its equal. The others had, even Hughie and Davina, who in their two short years here had become real children of the mountains.

Conrad said, 'It's too risky for you to go back tonight, Barbara. The creeks will all be up, the culverts may block and cause slips. Our own road out to the main road will be hard to negotiate.' He turned to Christabel. 'You know I pointed out that rough track above the East Portal the other day?' She nodded. 'I said that sometimes we had to use that if the creek between the Portals got blocked and overflowed the lower road? Well, it'll be well up by now.'

She looked amazed. 'Already?'

'We're so close to the watersheds. It was natural, of course, that Peer and Helga Josefsen, when they came here in 1869, should build back in here for some sort of shelter. It would have been better because of the narrowness of the pass between the Portals, to build nearer the lake, where it was logical for a road to run some day, but the primary need was for shelter from the elements. Imagine storms like this without the great shelter-belts we have all about us.' It was a sobering thought.

'I'll ring home in a minute,' said Barbara, 'Though they'll know we must have reached here by the time the storm broke.' At that moment the phone rang.

Conrad answered, 'We'd already decided they'd have to stay. Sorry to deprive you of Barbara's company, Elspeth, as soon as she has arrived, but your loss is certainly our gain. Of course there are beds and to spare. We'll kit them out for the night, and how about if they stayed on till late afternoon tomorrow, even if the slip's cleared? They'd never get out through the Portals, anyway.' He chatted on, then hung up.

'The road's already out. I don't think this will last, at this ferocity, but the damage won't be cleared till tomorrow.'

This had an extraordinary effect on the children. They leapt and capered about in glee to express their joy at such a break in routine. Conrad said, 'Look at them ... I've never known kids enjoy disasters so much! Serve you right if I work your fingers to the bone tomorrow, clearing drains. That's the difference between small fry and grown-ups ... a perfect illustration of the generation gap.' His eye fell on Barbara. 'Well, I'm darned! You're all sparkly-eyed too ... comes from being so long away from this territory, I guess.'

Barbara said simply, 'It'll be fun! It would be fun to her because she was a prisoner, with Conrad, behind the Portals. Here where she longed to be. Lucky Barbara! Christabel caught herself up on that wave of envy. She mustn't. Barbara was older than she was, and there was something about her mouth ... as if she'd served a long apprenticeship with pain. Oh, how stupid! That was what being a writer did to you, your imagination ran riot. If it had been as painful as all that, to carve those lines, Barbara would have followed Conrad to the crowded environs of a big city. Just as her ancestors, and his, had come to a wilderness where not even a road led north or south, east or west. They'd even had to break in a bullock-track, with their dray. Christabel knew, with a stab of painful certainty, that *she* would have followed Conrad anywhere, had he loved and wanted her.

An hour later the rain had stopped, though still the sound of waters pouring down the heights sounded, and gazing west they could see great rocks loosening from the hillsides, to crash down into the valley. The men and Conrad fared forth, on the horses, to see if any important culverts had got blocked when boulders were tumbled in. There could be major scourings-out if they weren't cleared. 'You'll let me come, won't you?' pleaded Barbara.

Christabel couldn't help a quick, beseeching look at Conrad. He made a rueful mouth. 'Sorry, I dare not risk it. You've come on a ton, but not on hillsides like this. Barbara's been riding round this terrain since she could walk. Anyway, Christabel, Jonsy'll be glad of your help in an outsized meal. The kids can help ... peeling potatoes and carrots.'

She watched them go with longing in her heart. Oh, well, on with the task in hand. Vegetables would be no trouble, but what about meat? They had only enough in the fridge for themselves. It would take to long to thaw out the cuts in the deep freeze.

Jonsy laughed, 'Not to worry, girl, this is the time I take out something from the emergency shelves ... cooked casseroles, and gently thaw them. That's what they're there for.'

'I hope this lasts and lasts,' said Rosemary with relish. 'With a bit of luck we could get three days or so over here.'

Christabel didn't wish it. She thought Barbara was lovely. But she didn't want her here, sleeping beneath this roof, as well as teaching under it. Barbara would be out with Conrad in after-school hours, riding round the estate, being knowledgeable about all matters of mountain farming ... Christabel would be shut up in his study, typing up what he'd accomplished so far, of his current novel. Not an enchanting prospect!

CHAPTER NINE

DARKNESS, because of the storm, fell more quickly tonight. Davina's room and Hughie's were twin-bedded ones, and a fold-up bed was put in Hughie's for young Angus Macandrew so he could be with Hughie and Iain. Barbara was given a small guest-room—for sure Thunder Ridge had elastic sides.

There had been times as more settlers had crowded into the Mackenzie, Jonsy said, when huge parties had been the order of the day, some people driving up to forty miles in open traps and gigs, and of course there'd been no thought of driving back when the feasting and dancing had ended.

Bed-rolls had been laid all round the woolshed walls, the women and children had slept in the house, packed in tightly and cosily. 'Later, I was one of the children, with my brothers and sisters,' said Jonsy. It started a flood of reminiscences, with Bluey and Shaun egging her on. It resulted, as might be expected, in the two of them saying, 'What's wrong with a spot of dancing tonight, three men, three girls?'

Jonsy blinked. 'Stop blarneying around! I might keep up my swimming, but dancing I've not done this last five years. My Nat never liked dancing, only endured it.'

Conrad laughed. 'Don't let her put you off. She's still got a light foot for tripping the measures. They had an old-time dance up at the Hermitage, Lancers and all . . . she had to show some people how to do it, and danced them off their feet. But we'll have to let Christabel decide whether we dance or not. She ought to be dropping on her feet. I didn't let her get to bed till dawn this morning. Oh, look at her . . . blushing again! It's all right, chump! I'd already told the lads what a sport you were over the proofs . . . going on long after they turned it in. I told

Barbara too. But if you want an early night, Christabel, we'll dance another night.'

The browny-green eyes danced. 'I won't stand for concessions being made because I'm a Londoner . . . if you ones from the Mackenzie can keep up a pace like this, for sure I can. Ever since I first saw that ballroom, I've wanted to see it in use. We may lack the sweeping gowns and what-have-you of the Edwardian era, but at least we can try it out.'

Conrad glanced at the warm pants they'd all donned and said, 'Nevertheless, damsels, you included, Jonsy, are going to get yourselves into more feminine garments than those. When we've done the dishes we'll run a mop over that polished floor, put a light to the fire in there, while you're changing, and we'll have a rare night of it, though not too late a one in deference to my new amanuensis. I've already mapped out a day for her tomorrow. I've got miles of things for her to look up. I've got my new book in my mind, but that's about all. If only my next book was set here, but it's to be Bay of Islands. I know it well enough, but I must have facts and figures beside me for quick reference as I write. Good lord, what's that?' he exclaimed suddenly. 'Nobody could drive up here on a night like this, surely?'

A thundering knock had sounded at the verandah door. They all rushed after Conrad. 'Curiosity unbounded,' he said to them over his shoulder. He pulled the door open and there stood a bedraggled figure, slight, tall, bearded, with a pack on its back. Conrad stepped out, caught him by his elbows and drew him over the threshold.

The figure pushed back wet locks from his forehead with limp hand. 'Sorry about this . . . I hadn't long left Glentanner Camp when the storm caught me. No shelter for ages . . . and I was drenched in five minutes. Then I found an old tin shed, but it had only three sides. I couldn't stay there more than a couple of hours, so I made for here. But your drive's longer than I thought . . . and under water between those two hills, so I had to climb. There's a girl staying here I met on the train.

I thought I could——'.

Christabel exclaimed, 'The student!'

Jonsy said, 'Gordon Million. Into the warmth wi' him. Get a hot bath running, boys, and Conrad, you get a change of clothes. Bluey, make it the downstairs bathroom. Shaun, there's a packet of mustard in the cupboard next my stove. Put plenty in. I'll heat up some soup for him to have first.'

In no time Gordon Million was rigged out in warm trousers and a big fisherman-knit jersey of Conrad's. It was ludicrously large on him. He was sitting up at the table presently, mopping up another bowl of bacon-and-barley soup, and then what was left of their casserole and apple crumble. He had more colour now.

'Good thing you kept moving, Million,' said Conrad, 'though I take it you're a seasoned tramper. Good thing too that you turned in here. The road's cut farther on.'

'I was going to call in anyway ... thought I'd like to see my train companion again.' Gordon Million grinned at Christabel, and she gave a polite smile back.

Bluey shook his head. 'Fast worker, this girl. Lands in New Zealand one day, and has a trail of fellows after her in no time ... striving through a blizzard, no less.'

She just had to take their raillery, but was inwardly rueful. Conrad had only just, she suspected, got over thinking she and Lisa could be birds of a feather. She was glad their waif of the storm elected to stay in a big armchair beside the kitchen range. He certainly wouldn't feel like dancing.

She took Barbara to her bedroom and opened her wardrobe. 'We're just about the same height and build ... you might be a little slimmer, that's all. There's this pink ... an obvious choice for you, I'd say, with those brown eyes, or there's this blue ... isn't it absurd of those men to insist on us dressing up?'

Barbara laughed. 'They're like that up here ... weeks in working clothes when the pressure's on, then whacko ... a celebration for no reason at all. Which is fun. Christie, I'd love to try that blue. For some reason, I've not worn blue much since I grew up. Isn't it lovely? A sort of shadow pattern, and what lovely draping. That cowl neckline in all those folds is just gorgeous.'

It was indeed, on Barbara. She said to Christie, 'Don't you want to wear it yourself?'

'No, for some reason, I regretted buying it. It's not quite me. But it's certainly you. I've only worn it once. I'm going to wear this white one. It's got a tiny bolero, so I won't feel it's out of kilter with the weather as I would wearing a wide-necked, sleeveless dress without a jacket.'

Christabel wondered if Conrad would remember that leafy spot on St Catherine's Hill ... would remember he'd said, 'I like a woman in a white dress on an English summer evening.' Would he think he liked her just as well in it on a March evening in the Antipodes?

She needn't have worried, he didn't mention it. He was crossing the hall at the foot of the stairs as they came down; he looked up, said, 'Why, Barbie, how beautiful you look ... I don't think I've ever seen you in blue before ... how clever of Christabel!'

Barbara gave a ripple of laughter. 'That sounds as if you've never thought me beautiful before. But never mind, Conrad darling, I'm always so grateful for a compliment, I'm not too choosy about them.'

When Conrad had said the two young girls could stay up and dance, they'd been rapturous, but Iain had said hastily, 'Not for us, at any price. We'll play Monopoly in our room, thanks,' and had been allowed to.

Davina and Rosemary had spurned the idea of dressing up in frocks, but had discarded their trews in favour of wrap-round corded skirts, which fitted anybody, they informed the company, and had Indian muslin blouses on that Christabel had bought Davina in San Francisco. She looked at the two eleven-year-olds and realised that in two years they'd be into their teens and on the threshold of womanhood. It gave her a pang, and she thought of Lisa, gay and pretty, with her bright copper hair and vivid topaz eyes at fifteen, with all her life before her.

Now she was gone and had left only heartbreak behind her ... a disillusioned husband, a little boy who was recovering quickly, and a darling daughter, who was now reserved where once she had been outgoing.

However, now wasn't the time to dwell on these things. Some of the dances had to be up to the minute to please the two little girls, and Bluey and Shaun quite enjoyed them, and one thing about those dances, it didn't matter that the numbers were uneven, but Conrad insisted on them learning some of the old-time dances too ... and was so understanding with them, so patient and tender, she wondered anew at the complexity of this man's nature. But then he was happy tonight, with Barbara home.

Bluey and Shaun, like most country boys, were excellent dancers. Shaun said engagingly, to the top of Christabel's head, 'I reckon Conrad could have us permanently now there's company like this round Thunder Ridge ... you and Barbara.'

Conrad, circling with Jonsy, said, 'Suits me. Gerry Meekham's going up to Dragonshill next month. He thinks it'll be even more exciting than this—more off the beaten track. We could take two more hands very easily with Rogan out of circulation. He'll be back up here before too long, we hope now, but he'll be confined to office management for some time.'

Gordon Million had revived and came in, began to enjoy himself. Conrad had no more dances with Barbara than he had with Christabel. She told herself she was a fool for so loving being in the circle of his arms, then let herself go, dreamily imagining there had been no conflict setting them against each other, ever. That there had been no harsh realities between those enchanted evenings at Tintagel and Winchester, and now, limbs moving in close rhythm with each other, his face an inch from hers, his breath warm against her cheek ... the nearness of him, the dearness ... the whole male attractiveness. She was glad the lights were low. They had turned on only three of the wall sconces, the rest was firelight flickering on these walls that had seen over three-quarters of a cen-

tury of fun-making. It had been built on in 1900 to celebrate Helga and Peer Josefsen's fortieth wedding an-
niversary. It had seen their fiftieth, and, surprisingly,
their diamond wedding . . . they had by then seen their
grandsons return from World War One, and in reaching
that sixtieth milestone, had made it a thanksgiving ball
for their safe return. They had died within a few weeks of
each other not long after. As these things were recalled
between the dancing, Christabel felt as if she had known
Peer and Helga, could hear their soft voices, with the
island tones of Orkney, and farther back of Scandinavia.
Pity their names hadn't been carried on by their descend-
ants. How lovely to have a small Peer and Helga growing
up here. She suddenly grew hot-cheeked at where her
thoughts were leading her. Conrad looked down on her,
and noticed; she had no idea why, but he chuckled. She
turned her head swiftly against his chest.

He said, in a low voice, 'I like a girl who blushes. It
means she's not as hard-boiled as might be thought.'

'What do you mean?' she queried.

'Never mind. Nothing controversial tonight.'

Christabel went on thinking about this ballroom, this
homestead. Here Conrad's sisters' wedding receptions
had been held . . . unions, according to Jonsy, that were
very happy and stable. Oh, yes, it had been a happy
high-country station till her sister had come here. But
right now, she must hold any dark thoughts like those at
bay, content with being here in Conrad's arms, drifting
dreamily to the slow music on the record player . . . drifting, drifting, steps matching perfectly, it was like being on
a cloud . . . as if one's feet didn't touch the floor . . . all of
a sudden there was a shout of laughter, and as from a
distance Conrad's voice, 'My partner's gone to sleep on
her feet . . . honestly! Oh, the poor girl. I bet no English
boss ever worked her so late she fell asleep dancing the
next night!'

The next moment she was being held tightly in case
she crumpled up, and gently steered over to a rather
elderly divan against one of the long walls. He slipped his

hand under her knees, lifted her, put her gently down against the cushions. She lifted her heavy lashes, stared up straight into the blue eyes, and had the craziest feeling that his look isolated them from the rest of the room, from the teasing laughter that was going on.

Bluey was saying, 'Can't be much of a heart-throb, can he? Maybe I'm not either, but no girl's ever gone to sleep when I've been dancing with her. It beats all!'

Christabel's lips curved into a smile. 'I'm afraid it does beat all, Conrad. But don't take it as an insult, it was only sheer exhaustion ... the late night ... but I loved doing it ...' her voice trailed off. She said confusedly, because he had his face so close to hers, 'I think I'm talking in my sleep, too, take no notice of me, please.'

His well-cut mouth quirked up at one corner in a way it had. 'I don't know. It makes better hearing than Bluey's nonsense. I like it.' None of this could be heard by the others. The room was too wide, they were laughing.

She sat up suddenly, bumping her head against his. 'I can't sleep here—I won't. And I just can't stay awake I'm afraid. No, I don't want a nightcap, thanks, or anything. Barbara, I'll put a nightgown and slippers and dressing-gown out on your bed. Goodnight, everyone. I shan't know another thing till morning.'

In that she was quite, quite wrong, because after three hours she woke and her mind came fully awake in a matter of seconds. A pity, because she would much rather have stayed dreaming, for in that dream there had been no jarring elements, no treachery on Lisa's part, no deception on the part of Tod Hurst ... Tod-cum-Thaddeus-cum-Conrad ... just a sunlit valley circled with great classical mountains, where harvest was gathered in with never a hint of storm ... where she and Conrad loved each other. Only a dream, but what a pity to waken.

How this old house creaked at night! Did friendly ghosts walk there? Was that Peer's footsteps coming upstairs? He would have a candle in his hand and he was coming up to his Helga in the big bedroom that had been the first room added upstairs. They wouldn't have had electric bed-lamps overhead for reading . . . they would have done their reading downstairs, by the light of kerosene lamps, soft and intimate. But that bedroom would be the centre of that man-woman world, the one parents lived in apart from their children, that world of tendernesses and caresses that was a blend of spirit and flesh and far removed from some of the ugliness of the substitute permissiveness of today. Helga and Peer would have been friends and lovers, she was sure.

There was that faded old photo of the two Jonsy had shown it to her. Not a posed picture; this amateur photographer had caught them laughing together. Jonsy had said, 'My mother and father knew them, of course. She worked up here before she married, and though neither Helga nor Peer were young then, she said Helga always went eagerly to meet her man when he came in from the paddocks, as if he'd been away down at the coast for days as he had to in the early years here, leaving her alone. Helga never walked when she could run, right on into her sunset years.'

Christabel smiled to herself. Helga had become a real personality to her. The stairs creaked again. She lay in a happy daze, re-living the past of this darling house.

Half an hour later she realised she wasn't going to sleep again, and now thoughts of the real situation here were beginning to intrude. Oh, stop it, Christie! she muttered to herself. Conrad doesn't resent you now. You've proved to him that if he's going to keep on writing up here, he needs someone like you. You're on his payroll. You can feel secure now. What more do you want?

But she knew the answer to that only too well. She might as well read. Nothing like reading in bed as a preliminary to sleep. Oh bother, that Ngaio Marsh she was reading was downstairs. She'd go down to the kitchen to get it. No doubt all the inhabitants of this house were flat out to it tonight. Except those friendly ghosts she had imagined on the stairs . . .

She drew on her velvet gown, thicker than the glamour one she had given Barbara, thrust her feet into lambswool slippers, stole down the first flight. The storm was well over because a shaft of pure pale moonlight was shining in through the landing window and she could even see the brilliance of stars with never a cloud to dim them.

Then she put her hand on the kitchen doorknob, she froze in her tracks. At the end of that passage was the big sitting-room, and beyond the open door of it was a shaft of light from a standard lamp, the only one switched on, and just within one edge of that beam of light, two figures were standing, locked together.

One was Conrad. He had a tweed dressing-gown on. The other ... Barbara! Barbara in that flimsy peachy wrap Christabel had left out for her. His arms were right round her, her head was pressed into his shoulder, one hand of his stroked the back of her head. Christabel sensed Barbara was weeping. Then Barbara lifted her head a little, gave a hiccuping sob and said, 'Oh, Conrad, it's been so long, so long! I just existed in Fiji. It wasn't me at all.'

He said in a low tone that was still audible to Christabel, turned to statue-like stillness, 'I know, I know,' and his voice was infinitely compassionate. He patted the back of Barbara's head, said, 'But it's over now. Remember that. Oh, sometimes we make such fools of ourselves, make such mistakes, but as Mother's so given to saying, we so often get another chance. Take your book, Barbie love, and read yourself to sleep, and don't forget, tomorrow starts a whole new era.'

Christabel was terrified her rustle of movement might betray her, but if it did, she would pretend she'd just arrived, she'd jump as if startled. However, she managed to turn, to regain the stairs, and by keeping to the edges got up without a single creak giving away to the two downstairs that somebody else was abroad.

She glided across to her bed without switching on the light or closing her door in case it was heard, got into bed and turned her face to the wall. But no tears came. So much for dreams! The reality was downstairs. Barbara had come home in every sense of the world . . . a true daughter of the misty gorges.

Next morning she heard voices from Barbara's room and supposed Rosemary had gone along to her cousin's room to talk. But as she passed the girls' door, she saw Rosemary still fast asleep, and Davina's bed empty. She halted at Barbara's open door. There was Davina in with her, talking ninety to the dozen. Christabel had always prided herself that jealousy was an unknown emotion to her. She had no time for it. It caused more than half the trouble in the world, she was sure.

But not once since she had come right across the world to help her sister's children had Davina done this. When she was younger, in England, it had been a custom. 'Mummy doesn't like me to do this,' she'd say, cuddling in luxuriously. 'She says she's too tired first thing in the mornings.' Now Christabel knew a scalding pang that was almost physical and hated herself for it.

She forced herself to halt in the doorway and say in mock reproof, 'Poor Barbara, a journey from Lake Tekapo yesterday, dancing half the night, and now you in her bed!'

Barbara laughed. 'Oh, don't worry, Christie, I've had a good sleep, even if a short one. My mind was so active last night I was downstairs in the wee sma's, looking for a book. Then I went forty fathoms deep!'

Christabel thought, but not because you read. No, because Conrad comforted you and you sorted things out between you.

She didn't blame Barbara for putting it like that. They'd tell the households in their own good time. There would be great rejoicing in both. Mount Hebron and Thunder Ridge estates united!

Barbara looked out of the window. She must have drawn back the curtains last night, or Davina had now. All storm clouds were gone. The sky had that ethereal, newly-washed look so often seen after tempest. The mountains were standing out like cut-outs in white plastic. 'Isn't it an enchanting morning, Christie?'

Yes, it was. But for Barbie, not for Christabel Windsor. It seemed strange the day could proceed in such a normal fashion, despite what had happened between bedtime and waking. The household chores were done, the poultry fed, and then with great gusto the children and Barbara and Christabel tackled the old schoolroom that had been unused for so long. Conrad had too much to do in the aftermath of the storm, but said tomorrow he would start Christabel off on her secretarial work instead of today.

Rosemary whipped round on him. 'We all call her Christie. Why don't you? Isn't Christabel a mouthful?— three syllables!'

He smiled that smile that made Christabel feel her bones were turning to water. She was never proof against it. 'I happen to think Christabel is too beautiful a name to shorten. It comes of being an author, I think. Names are so important to the writer when creating his characters.'

Rosemary flung her arms round him. 'Oh, I do love you, Uncle Conrad! You always talk to us as if we're grown-up.'

Conrad grinned, said, 'Well, you've already got all the wiles of Eve, so why shouldn't I?' then added, anxiously, to Barbara and Christabel, 'Don't throw out anything belonging to me from the schoolroom, will you? It's all grist to the mill, you know. I might have a beastly ten-year-old such as I used to be, nosy and interfering, getting in the way while my hero's running down a bunch of crooks, and I'll need my old exercise-books for gen.'

Rosemary said anxiously, 'But the boy will finally save the day, won't he, after incredible adventures?'

Barbara said, 'If they keep on like this, Conrad, you won't have to look for plots! But girls, you've got the wrong idea. His main aim is *to be credible.* I'll see nothing of yours gets thrown out, Conrad. In any case, I think all we don't want cluttering up the schoolroom should be consigned to the lumber-room, not the incinerator. If I run out of essay subjects, I might be glad to use your old ones.'

It was a mammoth task, but a fascinating one so that they couldn't speed up by being ruthless, and they made dozens of trips to the attic. Christabel had an idea she was going to find loads of material for her own writing in that attic. She blinked, aware that already she was thinking of writing with a New Zealand setting.

She couldn't resist dipping into some of Conrad's exercise-books whenever she found herself alone up there. She told herself it was because they revealed that even then, here was a potential author. It wasn't really. It was because they revealed Conrad as he was, under that tough crust he had shown her in that dreadful telephone conversation over leagues of ocean.

She picked up one that belonged, evidently, to his primer days. The governess of the day had set them writing out answers to questions she had written. She had framed them with a great understanding of small children. Christabel became very still as she read, absorbed. It was like dipping back in time, and looking into those schooldays of yesteryear . . . the schooldays of the man she loved.

One had been 'What things do you hate?' The small Conrad had written: 'Ground rice pudding, wars because they hurt people who don't want to fight, washing my ears because they're fiddly, getting splinters out of my feet, flies, overcoats and having to stop reading and put my light out.'

She turned the page. 'What things do you like?' She could just see the six-and-a-half-year-old Conrad scrawling away. His writing hadn't been as bad then as now, but still showed signs of haste to get down his thoughts. 'Things I like best are dry snow, horses, dogs, cats, Mum reading poetry to us on wet nights, pussy-willow catkins in the sun, the feel of wool when you part it on the sheep's back, and great-great-something Granny Helga's copper hotwater bottle, and choclit caramels that don't go away too soon, and being in the woolshed with Dad and riding on a steam train and fish and chips and seeing the sea.'

She had the most absurd feeling of wanting to burst into tears because she had never known that small boy. How absurd! Because what could it matter? Conrad belonged to Barbara, and though they had—must have—quarrelled and gone their separate ways for a time, now they were together again. She thrust the book deep under the others. It was a mistake to delve too deeply and to become emotional.

The Ministry of Works repaired the road, Gordon Million departed for home, mother, and varsity, and life settled into a regular routine. Barbara and the Mount Hebron children arrived every day at half-past eight and went home soon after three in the afternoons, bar the days they lingered on to play. Conrad seemed to be close to the homestead those days and he and Barbara went off walking by themselves sometimes. They must have decided that now was no time to announce an engagement. Perhaps they felt they'd like to have a celebration party when they did, and would want Conrad's parents here. At present they wouldn't want to leave Timaru, although Rogan was improving fast. In any case, they might not want too much fuss made, when his own love-life had fallen to bits. A certain serenity characterised Barbara, a quiet happiness. Perhaps, too, she found it rather fun to disguise her feelings for Conrad in front of everyone. She simply plagued the life out of him fixing up projects for the children outside the classroom, and was so blithe and gay no wonder everyone loved her.

Mary and Ninian, with old Joseph and Elspeth, often came over. Mary was sparkling-eyed about Christabel acting as secretary for Conrad. 'What did I tell you, Christabel, things have a way of turning out for the best if only we don't burn our boats behind us too soon, don't you think? What could be more ideal? Conrad is home here, where he ought to be, yet still writing his books. And Barbara is home too. I can begin to think time will heal things for Rogan now, too.'

That made it pretty evident the two families knew that

Conrad and Barbara belonged together.

March swung into April, and with April came Easter and already it was stingingly frosty in the mornings and gloriously sunny in the noontide and afternoons. Fancy, Easter in England meant a world waking to spring, but here every day the rowan berries grew redder, their leaves turned the most vivid colours, russet and gold and scarlet; poplars were living torches one week and bereft of leaves the next. They were putting out bread and suet for the birds now, except the berry-eating ones, and bowls of blackcurrant jam and water for the honey-loving ones with the nectar-brushes on their tongues.

Christabel knew by now that there was a house service once a month in one of the three homesteads along the road, that long road to the mountains . . . a very touching afternoon service in the big sitting room when it was Thunder Ridge's turn, with Conrad or Jonsy playing the old organ, beautifully kept, that Helga and Peer had imported from London in the 1880s. However, for Easter Day there was to be a combined service, irrespective of denomination, in the Church of the Good Shepherd, built out on a point of Lake Tekapo, the church whose altar window framed the classical mountains on the far side of the jewelled waters of the lake.

They had to be up very early. The paddocks, as they drove through the Portals, were glinting with silver frost, the air was like sparkling wine, the sky and mountains a poem of colour in purest blue and dazzling white with granite-grey jutting through where the rocks and crags were too steep to hold the snow. Right down the side of Lake Pukaki they went, hills carved out in strange contours all about them, huge sheep stations tucked into valleys so numerous Christabel thought she'd never get to know them all, then to the touching simplicity of the little church built high on a stark hillside, fashioned of the lake boulders, still with lichens clinging.

Such a mixed congregation, this glad Easter morning . . . station owners and hands, drovers, shepherds, trampers, with their studded boots, their packs left outside, and the beauty of the lake brought into the church worship, through the medium of the great altar window.

They were going to Barbara's friends' holiday house for dinner. They were business people from Fairlie and their house, Canadian ranch style, faced the lake. After dinner Christabel was out on the cedarwood patio trying to drink her fill of the vista before her. She found Conrad at her elbow as she turned. He said, taking the elbow, 'You and I are going for a walk through those trees—there's a splendid view, the best of all, from a sort of private lookout there. The others have seen it many a time.'

'But doesn't Barbara want to see it again?'

'No, we can't drag her away from Nancy, it's so long since they've seen each other.'

'I thought she stayed here on the way up?'

'She did, but Nancy wasn't here then.'

Christabel glanced up at the path between the trees. 'Just as well these aren't high heels.'

Conrad said, 'They're ideal for today,' caught her look of surprise and added, 'They're elegant without being nonsensical for high country. Like you.'

'Like me? What do——'

There was a certain suavity about Conrad Josefsen that was surprising. At times he was so much a son of the misty gorges, and the rugged mountains, at others you knew he'd lived a long time in cities, that his business was with words. He said now, 'You suit this terrain, Christabel. You can take the rough with the smooth, yet you always retain an air of elegance, very feminine. It's a gift. I believe the first Josefsen woman here had it—Helga.'

She wrinkled her brow at him. 'You are in a strange mood! If it's a gift, I don't consciously use it for my own ends like——'

His hand grasped her arm, roughly. 'Stop it! Don't bring Lisa into this. She doesn't belong to this Easter Day. She never did belong to the mountains, but her children do, and you do. I don't compare you with Lisa any more. I never should have done.'

Her heart soared up, just like that lark, singing high in

the heavens above the tussock. 'Is that meant for an apology, Conrad?' she asked.

'Yes, it was quite unjust. Only I was so sore for Rogan, and I felt responsible.'

'Responsible? You? How?'

'I brought a V.I.P. from the Commonwealth Office to Thunder Ridge. Everyone wants to see Mount Cook and the rest of our big fellows, some time. I was asked to bring this chap, show him homestead hospitality and the working of a big estate. I was to write him up, his reactions to all this. This one saw in Rogan just what he felt the London office needed for six months or so. The rest you know. I was starting to sell well, wasn't dependent upon my job any more, so I came home for that time to give Rogan the chance. Otherwise he couldn't have left Dad so near retirement. And it meant, in case you think I'm hinting at a sacrifice, I could flip over to the West Coast to Franz Josef Glacier in a Cessna or a helicopter, any time I needed to. I was writing that book you read on the trip. I pushed for Rogan to go away. And all this resulted.'

'I understand now,' said Christabel. 'I can imagine just how regretful you've been for Rogan's sake. But you mustn't whip yourself any longer. These things happen. I mean, if Rogan hadn't gone, and had, say, got caught in an avalanche on a climbing trip, round here, you'd have wished desperately you'd tried harder to get him to go to the U.K. Conrad, when I found out on Timaru railway station that *you* were Lisa's brother-in-law, *that Tod Hurst was*, I was really furious with you, felt it was inexcusable. In fact, until now, in the face, even, of much kindness to me and the children, I've still known some resentment about that. But I don't any more. I'd have felt just the same as you, for a loved brother whose life had been shattered. I would probably have felt it a good idea to find out more, secretly, about the type of person she was. Did you always have the feeling about her, Conrad, that she might prove unfaithful to Rogan?'

'Yes, because——' He stopped dead.

Christabel said, 'Please go on. It seems to be the day for plain speaking. And no offence taken or given.'

'Well, it so happened I did realise that if anyone with more money to offer came on the scene, she could grab at the chance.'

'Why? Were there other men ... other tourists, perhaps?'

Conrad was very reluctant, then, 'No, in fairness, I never saw anything like that. I wasn't here much when she was, but long enough to dislike her opinions. She said once, shortly after she came here with Rogan, just when I was handing back to him, why on earth didn't I have Rogan's money? That there wasn't much in newspaper work. Yet I lived in a city that could offer some sort of exciting life. I had still preserved my secret about writing books, you see. When they first arrived, I told Rogan I'd rather he didn't tell Lisa. Rogan's not analytical, he just accepted it. Lisa thought I went back to my job, but I didn't. I wrote full-time then. That sort of slant made me uneasy. I felt she liked Rogan's bank balance, not his way of life. But I began carrying on secrecy too far. Especially not telling you, on that trip, that I was related to you by marriage. Now you've been really big about understanding that. Not that it excuses it. But thank you, Christabel. Many a time I've wished I could undo all that's happened.'

He'd stopped, as if he'd thought of something. 'No, not all. Just most of what happened. I—I jumped to some very hasty conclusions. I've been proved wrong in so many of my assumptions I'm hoping to be proved——' Again he stopped.

She longed for him to continue. 'You hope to be proved ... what?'

He grinned. 'In this instance, second thoughts are wiser. I won't chance my luck too far today. Look—that walk, are you coming? I'm very conscious here that anyone of the crowd could join us any moment and we never seem to have much private conversation. There's always someone around.'

Christabel gave such a peal of laughter that, surprised, she clapped her hands to her mouth. 'Oh, dear, they'll arrive out here out of sheer curiosity to find out what's so funny if I don't take care.'

'I'll say . . . what was so funny anyway?'

'Just that we live in the midst of a mountain wilderness and you sound as if we're in a milling throng in Oxford Street most of the time!'

Conrad chuckled. 'Come on, wench, we don't need to go back through the room, we can go down these steps towards the lake, then climb from there to the track.'

As they entered the dark plantation, the track narrowed, forcing Conrad to lead. He put back a hand for her. She grasped it, then as it widened, tried to relinquish it, said, 'Don't, Conrad, Ba—someone might see.'

He sounded astonished. 'What matter? Don't be a spoilsport.'

That silenced her. The track levelled. He didn't let go of her hand, and she didn't try to free it. She couldn't. She was loving every moment of contact. What was it about this man that so stirred her to vibrant life? No one had ever made her so femininely aware of herself! Till now she hadn't been conscious of a physical need to be loved. She felt she had come alive.

They came out of the tunnel of trees to a rocky ledge above the lake. Though they could hear the sound of children's voices, happy and carefree, playing on the shore, and a silver-winged plane with scarlet markings was flying above, they were in a world of their own poised between the azure sky and the turquoise lake. Christabel brought her gaze back from that rim of snowy peaks on the far shore, to find him looking down on her very intently.

The jacket of her light woollen suit was open and blowing back and the cashmere top outlined the curves of her figure. The edging of white fur at the simple round neck of the jacket made her increasing tan glow with a dusky rose. The sun caught the golden lights in the short brown hair.

Unexpectedly Conrad said, 'How clever of you to buy an Easter suit exactly the colour of the lake. Pure turquoise . . . and how strange that your eyes have taken on that colour too. Most of the time they're greenish.'

The intensity of his look made her feel breathless. To hide it she said saucily, 'Aren't you observant today? Thinking of describing the heroine of your next book this way? It's a bit difficult for a mere male, isn't it?'

'Yes, but I'm finding you very helpful in that, remember? You made me add half a page in description of my Valancy, you wretch! You said as far as any reader was concerned, she was a nonentity in a blue dress.'

She laughed lightheartedly. 'I'll read that page very proudly when it's in print! I'll think smugly that there's a bit of *me* in Thaddeus Brockenhurst's latest thriller!'

He said slowly, as if it had just struck him, 'More than a bit, or so it seemed to me when I read it over.'

She was startled. 'Conrad, I didn't alter a word—honestly. I wouldn't dare do that to any author's work.'

He looked abstracted, as if far away from her in the world of his imagination—something she recognised as natural, from her father's abstractions. He came back to himself. 'Sorry, I suddenly thought of something. I didn't mean that. I know you wouldn't. You'd only offer a suggestion or a criticism. You have too much integrity to even sneak in a minor correction.'

To her chagrin, her eyes filled with tears. He put his hand under her chin, turning her face up towards him. 'Christabel, what is it?'

She bit her lower lip. 'Oh, just that, like Mary, I've over-active tear-ducts. Only that got to me. They're tears of relief. At first you seemed so—so doubtful of me. I felt I was under a cloud. That's the sweetest thing you could possibly have said to me.'

His lips twitched. 'Is it? Is it really? I could think of a few sweeter!'

She said, freeing herself and taking a lacy handkerchief out of her pocket, 'Stop it, Conrad! You're being foolish. I wasn't looking for compliments. I hardly know you in this mood.'

'H'mm. Pity. I've wasted a terrible amount of time being angry and suspicious with you.'

She felt a pulse beating at the base of her throat, knew she was experiencing all sorts of emotions that she must keep in check. Because there was Barbara, Barbara who had wept in Conrad's arms that painful night of storm.

He said abruptly, 'Want to know what I really brought you up here for?'

She lifted apprehensive eyes to his. What on earth——? 'No, I don't. So tell me.'

He looked as if he didn't like his task much. 'Barbara and I thought you ought to know, but——'

'But——?'

'I think you're big enough to take it. Barbara was sensitive about it, said any woman, under these circumstances, could feel a little slighted.'

These hesitancies, so unlike Conrad, were doing things to her. Barbara had said . . . what, oh, what had Barbara noticed? Christabel kept her tone cool. 'Do just tell me, Conrad. It could be nothing.'

He said, 'Well, here goes. It was good of you to come out here. Especially when I was so rough on you. Not that Barbara knows that. You came for the children's sake, then had to be told Lisa wasn't just missing, she was dead. You felt the children had a terrific need of you. As they had, but you found they'd identified completely with their stepfather's way of life . . . that Rogan is a true father to them, in everything except the tie of blood.' He paused.

Her voice was carefully controlled. 'Go on, Conrad. I accepted all that and was glad to find it so. Conrad, shall I make it easy for you? Are you trying to tell me that you know, and Barbara knows, that, apart from typing your manuscripts, I'm really quite superfluous here? I can take it.'

To her surprise Conrad caught hold of her elbows and shook her, quite roughly. 'Have you gone quite mad? We couldn't do without you now. We feel you belong to the Mackenzie Country. Jonsy said the other day she can't believe our incredible luck in getting you. The children *must* have someone of their very own, some link with their old life. Oh, dear,' he sighed, 'I've made too heavy weather of this! Serves me right. I thought at first Barbara was making too much of it, then she brought me round to her way of thinking. Listen, girl, and start to make sense of what this poor bumbling male is trying to say.'

Christabel said, staring, 'Go on.'

'You know you were worried because Davina had got so reserved, had gone in on herself? You felt you couldn't reach her? You hoped no psychological damage had been done to her because of her mother?'

She nodded; she couldn't speak.

'Well, Barbara is only worried lest you feel she had, in this respect, supplanted you, but she said to tell you it's a well-known fact that it's easier to confide in a stranger than to those near and dear to one. Davina, in an over-wrought moment, when Barbara was alone with her at Hebron, told Barbara she knew her mother wasn't just taking a lift with that man, that she'd deserted them.

'Davina said: "She was leaving Dad and leaving us to go and live in Hong Kong. Don't try to say anything different, Barbara, because I know she was. Uncle Conrad and Aunt Christie don't seem to want me to know. It's better Hughie shouldn't because he's too little, but I'm eleven and I know about these things." Barbara didn't hush her up or try to deny it. She admitted it and let her talk it out. She managed not to look appalled, she thought, when Davina said she picked up the hall phone one day to ring Rosemary and heard her mother making arrangements to meet Grosset and go. There was no way Barbara could lessen it for her, because Davina heard him say: "Well, put your luggage in the trunk of the car, and for heaven's sake lock it in case Rogan comes home early or the kids see you. Pity to bring too much, I'll buy you much more exciting things in Hong Kong." Her mother had laughed and said, "Better get used to the fact that I never travel light, darling. Anyway, the kids are playing with the shepherds' children and Rogan said he wouldn't get in from Number One Hut till dark. I'll be at the gate in exactly half an hour. I'll leave the car there, when you meet me. Better for me to wait for you than for anyone to see you waiting there too long."

'Davina went straight along to Rogan's office where her mother was phoning, and confronted her. She said to her, "I heard all that on the other phone. Don't go, Mum. Don't leave us! Don't leave Dad."

'Lisa had told her she was a silly little girl who didn't understand about grown-ups and that she wasn't leaving them for good, that when she got settled in Hong Kong she would send for them. Davina told her she would never leave here, never leave her stepfather. That got me. I thought it must have been one last desperate throw to stop her mother leaving.

'But it didn't work, if it was. That child saw her mother go. She wouldn't kiss her mother goodbye. And when she was gone she saddled her pony and rode up to Number One Hut and told her father. Ever since she's thought that if only she'd let him come home in his own time to find Lisa's note, that particular accident mightn't have happened. Fancy a child living with that, afraid at first that her stepfather might die! But Barbara's let her get it all out of her system . . . has made her see that if he'd got the news later, he'd probably have driven even faster. Only . . . we thought you'd been hurt enough, Christabel, and didn't want you upset because she hadn't confided in you, her aunt, who came thirteen thousand miles to try to help the children. And——' he looked away—'got anything but a good welcome at that.'

Christabel looked up, said brokenly, 'Oh, Conrad . . . as if it mattered who she told it to! All that mattered was that Davina should have confided in *someone*, and who better than Barbara? She needed to let it all out and become a child again, and she has, just lately, hasn't she, Conrad? As long as Davina was comforted, what do I care who did it? But . . . it was sweet of you both to care about my reaction.' Her lip trembled and she caught it between her teeth. 'I—I feel one of the household now, for the first time ever.'

Conrad stepped forward, put his arms about her and strained her to him, holding her face against his shoulder. The strength and vitality of him seemed to flow into her immediately. When she had stopped shaking at the realisation of all Davina had been through, she knew she must take this situation in hand. She raised her head a little, turned it sideways and said, 'Thank you, Conrad. I've never had a brother to comfort me. But you're a very good substitute—a compassionate man to damsels in distress. So thank you.'

He made an incredulous exclamation. He held her off so he could get his fingers under her chin, tilted it up so she had to look into his eyes. 'Christabel Windsor! Compassionate nothing! Brother nothing! I was holding you for the only reason a man *does* want to hold a girl . . . like that . . . sheer desire! I *want* to hold you. I *want* to kiss you. Like this! And go *on* kissing you.' He suited his actions to the words.

Bemused, Christabel didn't struggle. It was beyond her own desire. But presently he lifted his mouth from hers and raised his head. He was probably coming up for air, she thought dazedly. Then sanity returned and she said, 'Conrad, we mustn't! Just imagine if Barbara saw us!'

He boggled. '*If Barbara saw us!* Why, if she did, she'd clap!'

It was Christabel's turn to boggle. 'Conrad, you must be mad! What's going on? I mean . . . well, that night of the storm. *I saw you.*'

'*You saw me?* What the blazes . . .? Of course you saw me. You saw lots of other people too. I was dancing with you, remember?'

'I don't mean then, I mean in the early hours of the next morning. No, let me finish. I don't mean I thought there was any hanky-panky about it . . . you *must* believe that. Even if you *were* both in your night things. Oh, don't look like that! Let me finish.'

He had muttered: 'Hanky-panky? Night things?'

She said firmly, 'I woke up and couldn't get back to sleep. I went downstairs for my book and just as I got my hand on the kitchen door-knob, I saw you and Barbara. There was just one small light on. And you were kissing her. She said it had been a long time, that she'd just existed in Fiji. You said it was over now, that sometimes we make mistakes, make such fools of ourselves, but occasionally we get another chance. And you called her love and told her to take her book and read herself to sleep and not to forget a whole new era was starting.'

She could have sworn there was laughter behind his eyes when she gulped it all out and looked up. But he nodded very solemnly, 'Yes, I did. You've got it all word-perfect. So what?'

Christabel brought her hands up, clenched them into fists and thumped him on the chest in her exasperation. 'So what? So I've been expecting you to announce your engagement any time, only I realise that with Rogan in hospital and so many dreadful things having happened, you're biding your time. It's just not fitting to expect people who've had such an upset to rejoice with you, I suppose. I can understand it. I suppose years ago Barbie didn't want to leave her mountains to live in Auckland with you . . . but now you find you can go on writing at home . . . so she can have the best of both worlds.'

'Which are?'

'You know what I mean. Writers aren't obtuse.'

'I don't know. I was singularly obtuse last year in England, and I've paid for it since. Which two worlds?'

'You . . . *and* the mountains.'

'I see.'

'But *do* you see? All you want is within your grasp and you're idiotic enough to kiss me—like that!—and risk Barbara coming up here to find out how I've taken the news about Davina and seeing *that*!'

Conrad put his head back and laughed and couldn't stop laughing. Christabel could have smacked him. 'It's not funny!'

He tried to sober up. 'But it is. You called *me* obtuse—a

case of the pot and the kettle. Besides which, you had the
solution in your own words earlier when you called me a
compassionate man to damsels in distress. That's what I
was being to Barbara that night. Not what I was just now
... when I kissed you ... *like that!* I only kissed the tip of
her ear! I'd crept down because I thought one of those
wretched kids was raiding the fridge. And they'd had
more than was good for them already. And here was Barbara, all forlorn.

'Christabel, haven't you guessed? I didn't want to discuss it with you when Lisa had just gone, come to a tragic
end through her own folly ... she was, after all, your
mother's daughter. But that marriage was on the rocks
within six months of Rogan bringing her here. Barbara
had fled to Fiji because she couldn't bear to stay to watch
it and felt she'd only aggravate the situation. It so happened Rogan was surprised into saying something to her
one day—these situations do arise—about a hideous mistake he'd made. Barbie and Rogan were meant for each
other, only he was slow to realise it. That's why, if
Davina had to go to someone for comfort, I was glad it
was Barbara. It augurs well for a coming relationship.
I'm sure. Only it's too soon for anything to be said.' He
looked wistful. 'It *will* come right for everyone. This time
next year we may all feel quite different.' Suddenly he
shook off his concern for his brother and said whimsically,
'So next time, you bad girl, that I happen to kiss you,
don't spoil it by shrieking "What about Barbara?" in my
ear. It puts a fellow off!'

She couldn't take it in. She said hastily, 'You'll tell
Barbara I don't mind a bit about Davina, won't you?
And Conrad, you'll never tell her I witnessed that little
scene, will you? Or the conclusion I came to? What fools
we can be!'

His face went grim. 'Yes, what fools. I think we all do
it—jump to the wrong conclusions. Only at least you
didn't think the worst of *me!*'

'What do you mean?' she queried.

'I—once—thought the worst of someone else,' said

Conrad. 'Quite unjustly, I now believe.'

'You mean you've found out for sure about the person?'

'No, just that I've become more simple, less sophisticated. I can believe in innocence again. I'm trusting my instincts more.' He cocked his head in a listening attitude. 'Sounds as if the whole pack's coming up here. I guess if they were determined to join us Barbie couldn't hold them back. She's made a good job of keeping them at bay this long. I'll tell her we're on a different footing now. She's been wondering about us . . . knew something held us back. Christabel——'

She stopped him. 'Conrad, you're going too fast! I've only just discovered you aren't in love with Barbara. We've seen one disastrous infatuation. Make haste slowly, will you? Oh, dear, the crowd's getting near.'

It wasn't Barbara and her friends. It was a busload of tourists after the view. They were delighted to find a pair of locals at the Look-out. Their courier had sprained his ankle and had to let them make their own way up. Conrad began pointing out peaks, valleys where remote homesteads were tucked in, and finished up by inviting them to call in at the homestead on their way to Mount Cook. They moved down the track with them, delighted at the prospect of seeing a high-country sheep station not on their itinerary in New Zealand. As they turned from waving goodbye at the drive entrance to the chalet, Christabel said faintly, 'A whole busload. Serve you right if Jonsy boxes your ears!'

'Not Jonsy. She prides herself on being in line with the pioneer traditions of Thunder Ridge. Many a time when the first coaches somehow struggled through to the Old Hermitage, if they had a breakdown on the last lap, Great-great-granny Helga would put the lot up for the night, and if there wasn't enough bread for breakfast, she'd serve them oat-cakes and girdle scones made on the griddle over the open fire, after their porridge.'

Davina was sitting on the arm of Barbara's chair, leaning against her shoulder, but she shot off as Christabel came in, said, 'Oh, Aunt Christie . . . what do you think? Dad just rang up. They let him go to Granny's place for Easter to see how he could take it and if he's all right he can stay there and just go to the physiotherapist each day with Grandpa. He had a long talk with me, even on long distance. Says he'll be home in two shakes of a lamb's tail now. He wants us all to go down to Timaru next weekend. The shepherds can look after the place.' She hugged her aunt.

Christabel said, 'And I can keep the home fires burning.'

Davina said quickly, 'No, we're all to go. It's arranged. Barbie too. Dad said he was disappointed you couldn't get in to see him when you arrived, but he knew you wanted to get up here to us.'

Christabel caught Barbara's eye, and smiled, and there was a radiance in her smile. Things were coming right, not only for Barbara. She went across, dropped down beside Barbara and said, under cover of the chatter, 'I owe you a lot, Barbara . . . Davina is herself again. And so, I think, is Rogan's future.'

CHAPTER TEN

THAT weekend in Timaru was a surprisingly happy one. Christabel's hardest moment was meeting Rogan, seeing the lines on his face drawn by more than pain, yet knowing he was recovering in spirit as well as in body. He was especially good with Davina, and she realised that the experience they had shared when Davina had gasped out the news to him had drawn them very close. But then they had been good pals from the very start.

Christabel said to Jonsy, when they were alone, 'If I'd known how well cared for the children were, I mightn't have hurtled across the world the way I did.' They were walking round the Timaru garden, picking flowers to take back to the homestead, because up there, against the big fellows, frost took the late autumn flowers almost as soon as they bloomed.

Jonsy took a look at her slightly averted face, picked some lavender, twisted some wire round the stalks and said, 'Never be thinking it wasn't necessary, lass. You're what's wanted to keep Conrad at Thunder Ridge. Sheep and the mountains are in his blood as well as the itch from writing he got from old Thaddeus, and since you've been at the homestead, that lad's been a different person. He's never been quite settled before.'

Christabel grew very still, said quietly, 'Any man working as hard as Conrad is deserves a secretary.'

Jonsy said drily, 'Any man working as hard as he is deserves more than a secretary. That wasn't all I meant. It warms my heart to see my lad so happy.'

Christabel said hurriedly: 'I like hearing you say, "my lad," about Conrad. I thought it was lovely when he told me once that Rogan was in spirit very much your son because you brought him through a very critical infancy. But I've always thought you must love Conrad just as much.'

'Aye, that I did. All four of them. They filled a need. Conrad may seem self-sufficient at times, but he's not really. Although he was the younger brother, he was somehow the one who made things easier for Rogan. Except in one thing, of course, and no one could in that—except, now, Barbara. You'll have noticed how things are there?'

'I have. I think it's sweet. I hope the next few months pass very quickly for them.'

'But Conrad has needs beyond others. I canna express myself as well as you, lass. I'm not a writer like Conrad. But, Christabel, don't be letting the fact that your half-sister brought so much trouble to this family come between you and Conrad. Don't have any ideas about slipping away where you came from because of it.'

Christabel said, 'Jonsy darling, I don't know what to say, except that I want what's best for everyone. I don't want to be a permanent reminder.'

Jonsy put an affectionate hand on her arm. 'I don't think you'll be allowed to make up your own mind on that, love. Just take a day at a time. But how I missed the girls when they got married and moved north! You've made up a lot of that loss to me. I need you here too.'

In the succeeding days Christabel knew she was just letting things drift. Life on a farm had such a rhythm . . . just as night followed day and seasons followed seasons, and brought their own tasks, seeming to dovetail into each other, so this new understanding with Conrad seemed right and proper. She was grateful to him that, as she had asked, he was making haste slowly. Once he said to her, with a comic twist to his brows, 'Don't you think I'm being good? Letting you get to know me? Being patient, against my own nature?'

She had answered soberly enough, 'You are, and I'm grateful. Our family has caused you enough anguish. You aren't committed to anything, Conrad. We're marking time. No, don't kiss me. I can't think clearly under those circumstances.'

That had made him chuckle. 'I don't want you to

think. There are more ways of committal than thought
processes. All right . . . for the present. But some day I'll
call the tune. When my patience runs out.'

She was being wise for him, not herself. She knew so
well that there could be for her, only Conrad. But he *must*
be sure. There had been all those previous doubts of her;
she didn't want them to return. So day followed day, and
each one, she hoped, proved that the two of them, and
the life here, was right for each, and together.

Night fell earlier now, so Conrad spent some of the
evening hours at his desk. Sometimes Christabel sat up
there with him, most of the time she didn't, but busied
herself typing when he was out with the men among the
sheep or cattle. Quite often Christabel slipped upstairs to
her own room on the pretext of typing letters, and got on
with weaving her own current romance. Very soon now
her first book should arrive in all the glory of dust-jacket
and binding . . . she wasn't going to tell Conrad till then.
She even felt nervous about it. When she had written it
she had felt it to be good, now she had tremors. Might
he think it trivial? Perhaps a pleasant tale, but no more?
But it would give him a surprise, whatever his opinion
of it.

There came the day when Christabel was alone at the
homestead. Jonsy had gone across to Mount Hebron with
Barbara and the children when lessons were done. She
had driven her own car across for bringing them home,
after dinner, say about eight-thirty. 'I've left a chicken
casserole in the oven for you and Conrad and there's a
small trifle in the fridge. It might give the pair of you a
chance to really get some work done on the book. Run
along, children . . . you can go with the others if you like.'
When they were out of earshot she added, with a twinkle,
'There are some red candles in that cupboard over there.
I put them in the silver candlesticks this morning. Don't
have your meal in the kitchen, have it on the small table
in the dining-room, by candlelight. I've set the fire ready
for you. It's about time you put that lad out of his misery.
If eight-thirty's too early for us to return, give me a ring

and I'll delay things.' She burst out laughing at the look
on Christabel's face, and disappeared out of the door.

Conrad, Bluey and Shaun were up at Number One
Hut, repairing the sheep-pens up there. Conrad had been
disappointed she wouldn't go with them. It was only too
easy to succumb frequently to his suggestions that she
ought to see such and such an aspect of farming in the
high country, seeing she was doing his typing for him.
She'd said, mockingly, 'So far, no book I've been engaged
on in either proof-reading or typing has had a mention of
farming.'

'I mean future books,' he'd retorted. Nevertheless, as
she had watched them ride off, the sun shining on
Conrad's fair head, she had longed to go. But in the hours
they had been away she had managed a wad of typescript
for him.

But now she would shower and change and make the
final preparations for the meal in a leisurely way. Bluey
and Shaun were going off to Twizel to Shaun's mother's
for their dinner—there was a dance on down there.

Christabel went down for the mail and intended to sort
it at the house and then take it across to the cottages. The
phone rang. It was lovely, lovely news, but she did wish it
hadn't come just at this particular moment. But she'd
have to go. When people came thousands of miles to
give you a delightful surprise you felt they deserved
high priority.

The implement shed was over at Gillespies' so the men
would drop off there first. She would ring Mrs Gillespie
and explain. But luck wasn't with her. The youngest Gillespie boy answered the phone. 'But I could take a message,' he said proudly. Robert was always trying to catch
up to the others in matters of responsibility, but he so
rarely got the chance. Christabel told him that when the
men came back, he was to tell Conrad where she had
gone, that his dinner was in the oven and the pudding in
the fridge. That she'd got the mail, but hadn't had time
to sort it, and if he liked, he could come across with
Conrad and deliver it after that. And that she just might,

if possible, bring these friends back to spend the night.

Good job she had changed into this emerald green lightweight suit. She added a long rope of wooden beads she often wore with it, and matching studs at her ears, and a little more make-up than usual, for dining at the Hermitage. It didn't have to be too formal a dress, though you could go the whole limit if you wanted to, but this was a darling outfit. Conrad had liked her in it, and the Stennisons had never seen it. She caught up a fleecy-lined jacket for later.

As she got out on the road she wished she had left a note for Conrad. She could have suggested that he come up to the Hermitage and have dinner with Tim and Janice. She couldn't have waited for him in case he was late, because the Stennisons' time was short. Well, she could ring him from there.

A mile or two on she decided that in any case it would be nicest of all if they *could* come back for the night . . . they could see the children for themselves then. It would give them much longer to talk. Janice had been so excited, said they had just pinched this brief interval from the conference of travel agents at the Franz Josef, when they'd had the chance of skimming over the Alps in a helicopter. That they would be coming back later from a seminar in Christchurch to stay for a few days in Mount Cook Village, which would give them longer with her, then were going on to Queenstown and Milford Sound. This had been an irresistible temptation, to be such a short distance away as the crow flies . . . well, as a helicopter flies!

If they did come back to Thunder Ridge with her tonight, what could she give them for a savoury snack later in the night? For undoubtedly they would sit up till all hours, talking. Janice loved new recipes, and there was that delicious sort of vol-au-vent thing Jonsy had tried last week. The only thing, was they had used up the last of their frozen mushrooms. The autumn had been too dry, they needed rain, then heat to have them springing up in the paddocks. At that moment the store at the Glenfanner Motor Camp came into view. She would call in and see if they had any tinned mushrooms. She slowed up, crossed to the lake side of the road, and went in.

Conrad got back, to be met by the youngest Gillespie boy, full of importance, and glad his bossy older brothers weren't in. He rushed out, said slowly and deliberately, 'Christie rang up and told me to tell your dinner is in the oven and your pudding's in the fridge. She's gone to the Hermitage because a friend of hers, a travel agent, is staying there and she's going to stay the night. I'm to come over and get the mail. And are you taking the trail bike, 'cos I'd like to go pillion?'

He was completely unaware that this wasn't good news to his father's boss. He was dumped on the pillion, told to hang on tightly, and jolted across the tracks. Conrad strode into the office, unclipped the bag, tipped the mail out on the big desk there, sorted it quickly and said, 'If I put the mail for the others in a plastic bag, will you be very careful with it, Rob?'

Small Robert trotted off quite happily, full of pride, and quite oblivious of the fact that his message had completely devastated the big fair man he adored, and who now was staring blankly at his office wall.

Conrad came to himself, looked down on the mail, and hazily saw a package that had come airmail from London and bore the label of his own publisher. Surely not more proofs? He wasn't in the mood to cope with any right now! And it was doubtful that Christabel would be by the time he'd finished with her! He slashed savagely at the tight paper with a paper-knife and out fell one book . . . not a book by Thaddeus Brockenhurst. It was a romance, and in one corner was an oasthouse, with a man and girl standing near it, a dog at their feet. In Kent for certain, he thought numbly. Then the name of the author rose up and hit him . . . *Christabel Windsor*.

He couldn't quite credit it. He hurriedly opened the cover . . . yes, a first novel, by the daughter of another author, the late Hugh Windsor. Her second one was already in the hands of the printers. There was a photo of Christabel on the back flap, in that white dress that was his favourite. Conrad Josefsen was more angry than he had ever been in the whole of his life.

What a fool he was, what a gullible fool! Recollection of that day at Tekapo swept him about emotionally. He had actually apologised to Christabel because he had once practised a deception on her . . . he would have told her what unworthy thoughts he had entertained about her from the last day of that ill-fated tour round the West Counties, if those tourists hadn't come up the path. Well, thank heaven they had . . . otherwise she'd have accepted that apology too, with that dewy-eyed look of innocence that had so disarmed him these last few weeks. Imagine . . . and he'd had the smugness to think that he, unlike his brother, would never have been taken in by Lisa. Oh, they were two of a kind . . . it couldn't just have been Lisa's father who was a bad 'un, the mother must have been that way too. Oh, Conrad Josefsen was working himself into a fine fury!

He knew exactly what he was going to do. He was going to confront the two of them, Christabel and this man, and tell them in a seething but controlled way exactly what he thought of them. Praise the Lord Jonsy and the kids were out. No one to distract him, no one to deflect him from his purpose. And Christabel Windsor was going back to London!

He went upstairs, shaved, donned a light blue suit that had been ideal for Auckland, but which he had never worn here. He took care about selecting a shirt, tie, socks, shoes, yet he moved with speed because his temper was carrying him along. As he passed the office he caught sight of the book, picked it up, threw it in the back of the station wagon and drove off in a spurt of dust that wouldn't have disgraced a desert movie.

Conrad drove much faster than Christabel, and besides, when she got to the store, there was a long queue of campers wanting goods for their evening meal, and hunt as she could, among the fixtures, she couldn't find the tinned mushrooms.

Emerging at last, two tins clutched triumphantly to her bosom, she was amazed to see Conrad's car turn in off the road and streak up the rise. She stared still more when he got out. What elegance! Where could he be going? Oh . . . how truly delightful, he'd decided to come too. She rushed towards him. 'Oh, Conrad, how lovely . . . you're going to join us?'

Only then did she notice the thundery expression. It was so fierce she took a step backwards and almost dropped the tins. Conrad snapped, 'Yes, I'm joining you. Aye, I'm joining you all right! But we won't talk about it here. Leave the Triumph here. Give me your keys—I'll lock it. Get in the station wagon. We'll find somewhere short of the Hermitage to have this out.'

Christabel stammered in her fright. 'Th—the keys are in the car. I—b-but w-what—I left your dinner in the oven. You only had to take it out. You've never minded——'

He wrenched the keys out, locked the car and motioned to her to get in beside him. She moved like an automaton . . . she couldn't stay here, and have people come past them, fighting like this.

She almost choked her next words out: 'And don't drive like a bat out of hell, Thaddeus Brockenhurst! I don't want to risk my neck with a madman. And even though you're behaving like this I don't want you killing yourself or anyone else.'

He made a perfect gear change, slid smoothly down, waited till he was sure the road was clear and proceeded at a pace that couldn't have alarmed anyone and said through his teeth, 'Give me credit for some consideration of other people. You aren't worth risking anything for. But I'm going to get you some place where we can really have it out.'

A cold anger took possession of Christabel. 'I warn you it's going to be *some* confrontation. I *won't* be treated like this. You're going to have a lot of explaining to do to me, believe me! Roaring round like a Viking bent on vengeance! I'm not going to say one more word to you till we get to the spot where the duel is to take place!'

They both observed that grim silence till Conrad turned off into the mountains along a track that led into one of the secret glades of the bush. Christabel knew it because she and Barbara had taken the children there for a nature study walk one day. She said apprehensively, 'I'm not going in there with you.'

He snorted. 'Don't be ridiculous! What do you think I'm going to do? Beat you? We're having it out here beside the car. We've got to get off the road.'

She flung at him all the more fiercely because she *had* been afraid, 'Of course I'm not scared of you, but I look on that glade as a peaceful place, not for brawling. You may not intend violence, but you're about to tear strips off me, aren't you?'

'I sure am. And take that innocent wide-eyed look off! You haven't a hope of disarming me this time. I must be mad!'

'That I can believe,' said Christabel, matching insult with insult.

He said bitterly, 'I must be the biggest sucker . . . I had it in black-and-white and what did I do? Handed it back to you. Why? Because I thought I'd never see you again. But I did. And I then persuaded myself that you had integrity. That you might have been *tempted*, but you'd never have gone *overboard*. That was when I said that night we worked all night that I had the courage to go on! Oh, get out of the car, I can't do justice to it cooped up in here!'

She said between her teeth, 'Oh, you underestimate yourself. You're doing extremely well. Except that I haven't the faintest idea what you're talking about. Sure I'll get out. I need lots of air, fresh clean air, at the moment.' As she turned to get out something bright on the back seat caught her eye. Then her own name leaped up at her. 'What's *that*?' she demanded. 'Where did you get it?'

Conrad was out of the car and striding round to her side. 'That's just another example of your passion for secrecy. Why didn't you tell me you were an author? I only saw the publisher's label, and opened it. Why didn't you tell me?'

'For much the same reason you brought yours out under a nom-de-plume. Well, shyness actually. Surely you can't find anything sinister in that? I *was* going to show it to you when it arrived, but not before. And——' she choked a little—'I thought your need for someone to type your books while you substituted on the estate for Rogan was greater than mine. You won't believe that, of course. You don't seem to believe anything good of me, and I don't know why!'

Suddenly his voice lost its fire and sounded weary. 'Only because you don't know I *know all about it.* I hoped you'd put it all behind you, I'd almost forgotten it—I thought you'd turned your back on it too. But no . . . it was simply that the opportunity wasn't here.'

Christabel felt dazed, gave her head a shake, then said clearly and steadily, 'Conrad, tell me and get it over with. Even a prisoner in the dock knows what he's charged with. But let me tell you this: Whatever it is I refuse to let it spoil my evening. My best friend and her husband have just arrived at the Hermitage by helicopter from Franz Josef—as I told Robert to tell you! Janice is the dearest person in the world. She would be utterly distressed if she thought there was still trouble here, when I've assured her in letters that all's well. If she thought I still wasn't wanted. I was going to see if they could possibly come back with me to stay the night at the homestead. I wanted them to meet you, wanted them to see the children, know how happy they are in the life there. But I certainly won't now. You can leave me at the village. I'll get home somehow. I don't mean *home* anyway. *Home for me, evidently, is London.* I can't stay here. I've loved it and I don't think I'll ever be the same again, because I've lost my heart to the mountains, but stay I cannot . . . Conrad, what's the matter with you now? What are you looking like that for?'

He grabbed her by the upper arms, said in a low, urgent tone, 'What did you say? Your best friend? And her husband? And you were bringing them both back to stay the night with us? But I—I don't get it. Robert said a friend of yours had arrived at the Hermitage, that he was a travel agent, that you were going to spend the night with him . . .'

Christabel stared at him. 'Oh, no . . . oh no! I *should* have written a note. Only it was quicker to ring Gillespies' and wee Robert was so anxious to take the message. But surely you didn't believe that? How *could* you? You know me! Oh, I get it. *I'm Lisa's sister*. We're back to square one. I'm tarred with the same brush. Oh, how could you?'

He said, but quietly, intensely, 'I'll tell you how I could. Because I read part of that letter you wrote your best friend's husband when we were on that trip. Till then I'd loved you . . . and my only worry had been how was I tell you I was Rogan's brother and have you forgive me. And the maid handed me your letter pad. She said it was yours, but when I looked, it had Janice Stennison written across the cover. I thought she'd made a mistake, so I opened it to make sure. I thought it must belong to someone else. But when I flicked up the cover, your letter hit me in the eye. You know what a fast reader I am . . . I take in a line at a glance. It was horrible. I couldn't believe it. You said you couldn't live without him, that it was something you'd never dreamed would happen to you, that you could fall in love with your best friend's husband. How do you explain *that*, Christabel? How? And it came just the morning after that magic evening on St Catherine's Hill in Winchester. What about that, Christabel, even if tonight's little episode is whitewashed because his wife's with him . . . come on, *explain!*'

Suddenly Christabel's legs just wouldn't support her. The passenger door was open behind her. She groped for it, turned and subsided sideways on to the seat, her feet in their frivolous green shoes still deep in the grass where the heavy dew hadn't dried all day. She put her hands up to her face.

Conrad came nearer, tore her hands away, gazed in sheer amazement and said, in the most offended tone, 'You're laughing. *Laughing!* It's no laughing matter to *me*. I can't help loving you. I'm as big a fool as Rogan! *Stop laughing!*'

But she was helpless. She said, between gasps, that were only infuriating him more and more, 'Oh, Conrad . . . Conrad! You've brought the explanation with you. Oh, happy, happy timing! How ghastly if I'd had to send to our publishers before I could convince you.' She reached back, grabbed her book and began turning over pages feverishly.

She muttered, 'Oh, please, please God, let me find it quickly . . . please!' She stopped laughing. 'I never did, Conrad. I wouldn't. I never for one moment fell for Tim. Oh, here it is . . . almost word for word. Read it, read it, and when you have, get on with telling me what you said all over again. I mean about loving me . . .' He was still gazing at her, uncomprehendingly. She said, 'I didn't write that letter . . . at least only as far as I had one of my characters write it. Not even my heroine, but her cousin. Who was indiscreet and begged her cousin to get it back for her, which landed my heroine in a terrible tangle . . . but not half as terrible as this. What it landed *me* in! Jock Mennington, your publisher and mine, hadn't been satisfied with what I wrote first. It wasn't strong enough, damning enough. He thought I could make it more dangerous, more ambiguous. *And heaven help me, I certainly did!* His letter asking for the re-write reached me the day I was packing for that trip. I'd stayed with Janice, overnight. I'd forgotten a letter-pad, so she gave me hers. Read this page, Conrad, read it or you'll never believe me!'

He read it, looked down on her, dropped on the wet grass to bring himself to her level, put his arm on her knees and said, 'Christabel, Christabel darling, *you* said I was a fool, *I* said I was a fool . . . I *am* a fool, but if you could *know* what I've gone through! What I went through that morning boarding that coach in Winchester! We were surrounded by all those people. We had to sit side by side throughout that livelong day ... it was hell. I just cleared out, cut my visit short and went back to Auckland. I knew Rogan's marriage was folding up. I told myself I'd had a lucky escape ... Christabel, imagine if we'd never worked it out, never known ...'

She said, her eyes dancing, the corners of her lips curving up, 'Conrad, get up, you're in the traditional pose for proposing, it's like something out of *Lady Windermere's Fan*, but that isn't a carpet ... it's soaking! But don't let it interrupt ...' She stood up, as he stood up, then they reached out for each other and looked deeply into each other's eyes. Christabel could feel Conrad's heart thudding against her, then he put his face against hers, turned it to press his lips to her cheek, damp with the tears of her laughter, and so came to her mouth.

The sound of a strident and derisive horn brought them to awareness of the proximity of the road ... they drew back a little from each other, turned startled faces towards it, and saw a coach going at a snail's pace towards Mount Cook, with a row of interested faces peering out. 'Let's be sports and wave to them,' said Conrad, in high gig, 'after all, this started with a coachload, so it's all in keeping. Darling, let's go and tell your best friend and her husband that we've just got engaged to be married—and I'll slit your throat if you give them as much as a hint of how it came about, or that we ever met before you came to New Zealand. They'd snatch you up and fly back to England with you to protect you from such wild Colonial men!'

She was laughing again. 'It's that Viking strain. But I love it, I just hope——' She stopped dead.

'No need for prevarications now, my dearest love. You're blushing ... and you blush so beautifully, Christabel. Tell me, do your blushes rise up, or just fade downwards ...?' His eyes were on the deep low neckline.

She said, audaciously, 'You might know some day ... darling, do stop it ... there could be another coach. They so often come in at this time.'

'Who cares? And I know very well what you were going to say. You hope we have children with this Norse colouring. I don't, I'd like a darling daughter, with eyes that are sometimes browny-green like English beech-woods, or almost turquoise when she wears that colour, and goldy-brown hair with a ripple in it and a saucy way of setting a fellow back, a poor blundering fellow who's just been through hell. But come on, my love. Think of your best friend, and her wretched husband, coming all that way over the Alps in a chopper, to see you . . . they'll think you aren't coming.'

The mountain village seemed another world . . . by the time they got there the lamps were lit, the Hermitage was a hive of activity, beautifully dressed guests were in the lounge, Mount Cook was faintly outlined in silver by a moon that had been but a pale wraith of a moon in the twilight but now turned its light on too.

Christabel had renewed her make-up and her feet felt drier and warmer now because Conrad had turned on the car heater. She and Conrad came into the room; Christabel spied Janice and Tim at the far end, began walking towards them. Christabel's colour was high, her air eager. Both Timothy and Janice noticed that her escort, tall, fair, broad, had a possessive hand under her elbow.

Janice's pulses quickened. 'Tim, who can she be with? . . . She didn't say she was bringing someone . . . I wonder . . .' Then there was no time for more, because they were greeting each other.

Kisses over, Christabel said, 'This is Conrad Josefsen.' Janice caught in her breath, thought: 'Ha . . . the one she hardly ever mentioned in her letters . . . the one who didn't want her to come . . . H'm, she must have mellowed . . . I mustn't say a word, though.'

Timothy had no such inhibitions, he said, 'Good lord . . . you don't mean it? The one who told Christabel not to come? . . . It just goes to show!' Janice could have slain him.

Timothy, quite unperturbed, laughed and Conrad laughed with him. Conrad said: 'The very same—incredible, isn't it? I must have been stark raving mad. But

Christabel knows what a fool I am. And it doesn't seem to matter.' It made for easy acquaintanceship.

Timothy led them back to their low table, said, 'Now, what will you be drinking?'

Conrad's eyes began to dance in the old familiar way. 'Sorry if this sounds expensive, but it's got to be champagne. Christabel and I just got engaged half an hour ago.'

It was a wonderful evening. Conrad, of course, was known to the entire staff and management, and Christabel, by now, only a little less so. It became evident to the entire dining-room what the celebration was for, and they heard one woman say to her companion . . . 'I'm sure that's the girl in the green dress by the side of the road . . . you know, she was being kissed.' Conrad and Christabel looked at each other and collapsed into laughter.

Conrad slipped away to the phone and rang Jonsy at Mount Hebron . . . She said it didn't surprise her one whit, but she couldn't imagine what he'd taken so long over. And it didn't matter tuppence if the casserole was charred to cinders, she was only happy Christabel had friends from her other life with her to celebrate.

Conrad said to Christabel privately, 'And she never will know, either. She'd eat me if she knew how I'd behaved to you . . . you're the apple of her eye. It'll warm the cockles of her heart to look forward to another clutch of little Vikings to rear.'

Christabel said happily, 'Yes . . . small Helga and Peer. There are simply no other names, are there?'

Janice and Timothy decided to stay on at the Hermitage. 'We'll come out to Thunder Ridge in the morning. We fly back at two tomorrow afternoon, but we'll be here longer on our return. I know the night I got engaged to Janice I didn't want to share her with anyone. Oh, by the way, I'll just go up and get that book for you, *your* book, Christabel. It's just out in London. We thought if your copies came surface, you'd not get them for weeks yet.'

Conrad said smoothly, 'We just received an airmail

copy today, but it's lovely to have another. We'll send it down to Mother and Father. I think I can truly say that receiving that book when we did made it really a red-letter day, didn't it, darling?' The dancing blue eyes met the dancing greenish ones.

They drove home with the moon making a glimmering path of light across the bosom of the lake ... drove through the Portals, dark and shadowy, into their own small kingdom. Hand in hand they came up the terrace steps, paused to look with loving eyes at the distant scene before they must go into the lighted kitchen where Jonsy would be awaiting them.

There through the cleft in the nearer mountains reared the ghostly peaks of the Cloud-piercer. 'But tonight there aren't any clouds to pierce,' said Christabel happily and meaningfully.

Conrad drew her close. 'You're a true daughter of the misty gorges, aren't you, sweetheart?'

She nodded dreamily, held there in the strong circle of his arms, kissed him lingeringly and said, 'These are *my* mountains, *my* stars, *my* moon, and above all, my Thaddeus ... my dear, *dear* Thaddeus, the biggest fool in Christendom.'

HELP HARLEQUIN PICK 1982's GREATEST ROMANCE!

We're taking a poll to find the most romantic couple (real, not fictional) of 1982. Vote for any one you like, but please vote and mail in your ballot today. As Harlequin readers, you're the real romance experts!

Here's a list of suggestions to get you started. Circle your choice, <u>or</u> print the names of the couple you think is the most romantic in the space below.

Prince of Wales / Princess of Wales

Luke / Laura (General Hospital stars)

Gilda Radner / Gene Wilder

Jacqueline Bisset / Alexander Godunov

Mark Harmon / Christina Raines

Carly Simon / Al Corley

Susan Seaforth / Bill Hayes

Burt Bacharach / Carole Bayer Sager

_____

(please print)

_____

_____

Please mail to: Maureen Campbell
Harlequin Books
225 Duncan Mill Road
Don Mills, Ontario, Canada
M3B 3K9

POLL-1

There is nothing like...

Harlequin Romances

The original romance novels!
Best-sellers for more than 30 years!